MW01713105

The Year of Yearning

Jeff Harmsen

Best wishes,

Jeff Harmsen

Thanks for your support!

jharmsen2071@rogers.com

First Electronic Book Text, 2015

ISBN 978-0-9781168-2-8

All characters appearing in this work are fictitious. Any resemblance to real persons, living or dead is purely coincidental.

Published by Author, Jeff Harmsen

Newmarket, Ontario, Canada

Cover design by Jeff Harmsen

Cover image © by Jeff Harmsen 2015

Prologue

The Needler's condo in Mexico was supposed to have been completed in the summer of '77; here it was December 27th of that year, the fifth night of their Christmas vacation, and wires hung out of walls that were primed but not painted. Worst of all, the air conditioning had yet to be installed.

Damn it was hot. Bleeding beads of sweat hot. Dave Needler wore nothing but grey sport-shorts. The humidity had frizzed his shaggy blond hair. The strapping seventeen year old paced like a young lion-man, his meaty feet slapping and stomping the rusty-brown, tile floor.

In contrast to his angst, his stepsister sat near an electric fan, content to peruse the current issue of *Vogue* magazine. The first thing most people noticed about Laura Needler was her immaculate hair: downy streams of sheen black strands, draped thirty minutes down her hourglass figure, not a second more, not a second less.

The sofa she sat on was ornately designed with leafy vines and bright red flowers. As the fan blew her feathery hair slightly ruffled, it gave her an exotic air, like a Blackbird Goddess in a tropical breeze. Enthralled by a one-piece bathing suit, she held up a glossy picture and said, "Hey Dave, do you think I'd look good in this?"

"*I* don't know," he said without looking.

"Come on ya big *oaf*, take a look! It has a plunging neckline, the bottom is French-cut. What really sets it off is the sash: See how the tied ends fall to the side? It's like her thigh is peeking from a curtain."

"*Let me see?*" He glanced at the picture and turned away. "I like bikinis better."

"This is way better than a bikini! It's more chic, absolutely to die for. And it's black, so it matches my hair perfectly."

"Whatever you say. You're the fashion expert." He stepped into the front foyer and was suddenly captivated by an engraving on the back of an oversized oak door. The art work depicted *tercio de muerte*, the final stage of a bullfight, the bull's chin low in the dirt, its horns tangled in the cape. The matador was poised to thrust his sword between its shoulder blades, the traditional *Estacada* intended to slice through the animal's heart.

"You seem tense," Laura said, coming out of her *Vogue* trance, "What's the matter?"

"Is it fair we have to stay here, cooped up, while our parents go out all night? It's like we've been grounded for no reason." (She shrugged and flipped the page of her magazine.) He suddenly glared at her. "You know, my dad never used to take off on me like this, not when he was with my real mother. It only started happening when he got with *your* mom!"

"My mother has nothing to do with it! You're certainly old enough to be left alone for the evening; or do you still require a babysitter?"

"No matter how you twist it with your voodoo talk, my dad never used to take off on me like this, and now I'm so bored, I could go out and smack somebody—*anybody*—right in the chops, just for the hell of it!"

"*Voodoo talk*?" she said, laughing, "What do you mean by that?"

"You're like the witchdoctor on *Tarzan*. He's always messing with someone's head, like the time he cursed a native with a freaky straw doll, or when he turned himself into a black panther and led Tarzan on a wild goose chase."

"You think I use black magic to lead you astray? Is that what you're saying?"

"Not exactly…well, yeah, exactly! When we argue, you twist things around and complicate matters—you lead me astray with your voodoo talk!"

"Your boredom isn't that complicated. You've been spoiled your whole life, so you take these holidays for granted. I mean, here we are at a brand new resort, with gorgeous tans—although, I must say, I'm a lot darker than you are, see—" She held up her arm, fiercely proud of her bronzed, olive skin. "Not that it's a competition or anything."

He rolled his eyes and returned to the oak door where he mimicked the matador, an imaginary sword thrusting through *el Toro*.

"Think about our friends back home," she said, "They're half frozen, bundled up in coats and boots. I'm *so* tired of wearing boots, all winter long toe to heel tugs-of-war. I think Jeeves gets a kick out of helping me, as if pulling my boots off turns him on. Then again, who can blame him? I do have gorgeous feet!" She straightened her legs and admired the coral nail polish on her tanned toes. "Of course, some boots are harder to get off than others. Remember the knee-highs I bought in Toronto last year?"

"Yes, of course, I wrote it down in my diary."

"*You* keep a diary?"

"Cripes Laura, you're stunned! What do I care about your stinkin' boots?"

"My point is that we're lucky to be in Cancun. It's cold to the bone back home!"

"In my opinion, the heat here is worse than the cold." He paced with his beefy hands clasped behind his back. "At least if I were back home, I'd be stoned by now. I bet if we walk along the beach we'd find some locals who'd sell us a joint. Mexico's known for it. Ever heard of *Acapulco gold*?"

"I can't believe you smoke that stuff. I thought you were an *athlete*."

"Ha, that's a joke. Half the football team smokes pot. How'd you think I got into it in the first place?" He suddenly dropped to the floor and pumped out seventy pushups. Back on his feet and panting, he said, "Come on Laura, our parents will be out all night. Let's not waste another minute cooped up in this sweatbox!"

"Why don't you watch TV?"

"Yeah, that's why I came all the way to Mexico, to watch TV, something I could *never* do back home!" He went to the bar, removed the cork from a bottle of single-malt scotch and downed a couple belts. Then he ran tap water into the bottle to replace what he had drank.

"I don't think you should use tap water for that. Ever heard of *Montezuma's revenge*?"

"Don't worry. Alcohol kills the germs. What I really need is a doobie." He turned on the TV and plopped into a wicker chair. There was only one station, channel 5 from Mexico City. Through snowy reception, he saw a *saguaro*, the human shaped cactus, standing in the desert like a sentinel. An announcer belted out, "XHGC, channel 5, La imagen bonita de Mexico!" (The beautiful image of Mexico.)

The station soon aired a rerun of *The Brady Bunch*, the sitcom about an American stepfamily. Although the theme song was dubbed in Spanish, Dave sang along in English: "*Here's a story of a lovely lady, who was bringing up three very lovely girls. All of them had hair of gold, like their mother, the youngest one in curls.*"

Laura cringed. "Do you have to watch that?"

"This was one of my mother's favourite shows."

"And you wonder why your dad left her?"

"It was *your* idea to turn the TV on and there's only one station. He joined the chorus and sang with added vigor: "*THE BRADY BUNCH, THE BRADY BUNCH. THAT'S THE WAAAY WE BECAME THE BRADY*

BUNCH!" When the show started, he kept repeating the chorus: "*THAT'S THE WAY WE BECAME THE BRAAADY BUUUNCH*!"

Laura went into her room, then reappeared wearing earmuffs, the ones she had worn to the airport back in Toronto. The site of her wearing those fluffy, purple muffs, in the Mexican heat, cracked Dave up. But then he realized she wore them as earplugs to shut him out. He yanked them off her head.

"Hey!" she said, "What'd you do that for?"

"Truth is Laura, if I go out by myself, I'd look like a loser with no friends."

"Your dad would *freak* if we left. He scares me when he gets mad."

"What he doesn't know won't enrage him!"

"If you want to take that chance, go ahead. I'll never tell."

"Yeah, right, if I get caught alone, you'll look like Ms. Goodie-Two-Shoes!"

"Since when do you care what I look like?"

"Come on Laura, I really need a doobie. We'll score a joint and come right home again. You might even want to try it. Can you help me out this one time?"

She shook her head and lowered her chin. Her hair fell forward across both cheeks, a thick, soft barrier against him. He, in turn, stepped up to the oak door and pounded it with the bottom of his fist. It startled her. "*Take it easy*," she said.

He stormed to the sofa and towered over her. "I know what this is really about. You think you're too good to hang out with me!"

She raked a strand of her hair over her ear and looked up at him, her eyes dark and stern. "I don't *have* to go with you if I don't want to.

You're not the boss of me. If anyone's the boss, it should be me: I'm older."

"By three months, big deal! Look at you: Little miss prissy, can't get off your fat ass!"

"*Fat ass*? Right, Dave. Good one."

His insult was a losing gambit and he knew it. When it came to Laura's body, her confidence was more than bullet-proof; it was *ballet proof.* Although she never aspired to dance professionally, she loved what the classes did for her figure.

After drinking more scotch, Dave started playing with the bottle, flipping it in the air and catching it, a little higher each time, until, on his sixth toss, he fumbled it and the bottle smashed upon the tile floor. He glared at her: "*Now look what you made me do*!"

"Don't move," she said, "Stand perfectly still!" He rarely took orders from anyone but listened this time. She stepped into her sandals, retrieved a broom and swept the broken glass away from his bare feet. "Alright," she said, "I'll go to the beach with you. Give me a minute to change."

Dave used a dustpan and paper towels to clean the mess, then went to his room and pulled on khaki shorts and a red polo shirt. Restless, he paced in the living room, until finally, twenty minutes later, Laura came out of her room, radiant in a white sundress.

They skipped down two flights of stairs (the elevator not yet in service). Only a handful of other rooms were occupied at the Beach Paradise Resort. Once outside, gusts of wind tossed their hair about. "Doesn't this feel better?" he said.

"I have to admit, the condo was stifling hot."

Thunderclaps boomed out over the ocean; above them, the sky was clear. "A full moon tonight," he said, looking up.

"Like a spotlight from the heavens," she said, following his gaze.

Construction lights illuminated the skeletal concrete of one new hotel after another. "Can I ask you a question?" he said, "Why do you hate *The Brady Bunch*?"

"Because Dave, they're lame. They make step-families like ours seem weird, like we're all from *The Twilight Zone*."

They passed the glow of the last construction site and a bonfire materialized in the distance. "Over there!" Dave said, "Local yokels!"

Upon closer observation, they could see several Mexicans whooping it up, drinking hard liquor straight from a twenty-sixer bottle. "I don't know Dave, they seem creepy."

"Look how small they are; think they'd mess with the likes of me?"

She froze in wary contemplation.

"You don't want to be my own personal *Marsha Brady,* do ya? Come on, let's slum it for a while. We'll have a blast, you'll see."

Reluctantly, Laura followed him to the fire. The instant she reached the gang there she regretted it. Three generations of Mexicans, filthy, perhaps homeless, were getting drunk together. The oldest was a woman who looked to be in her seventies; the youngest was a kid who seemed to be in his mid teens. Four of the adults wore ragged blue uniforms, most likely from long lost jobs. The glow of the bonfire also flickered upon a little boy, off to the side, blanketed and asleep, nestled against a log.

Despite their rough exteriors, the saccharine scent of marijuana filled Dave with a delirious, kindred spirit. "*ALOHA!*" he belted out.

Laura said to Dave, "Where do you think we are, Hawaii? It's *hola*."

The Mexicans broke into laughter. A man in his early thirties staggered over. "Is okay señorita, I speak Americano. We like Americanos."

"Actually, we're from Canada," she said.

"American, Canadian; tomato, potato, what's the difference, Laura?" He reached out and shook the man's hand. "I'm Dave. This is my sister, Laura."

"I'm Bruno," the man said. He pointed to three adults sitting on Aztec blankets: "This my papa, my mama and my grandma." He introduced those standing beside him: "That my sister, Maria; this my brothers Lupe, Jose and Marco."

Dave shook all their hands. No way would Laura do the same: the thought of touching them—*whatsoever*—made her skin crawl! She clasped her wrist behind her back; but this posture protruded her breasts, so she quickly crossed her arms in front.

Bruno nodded to Maria, who hurried a swig of tequila, then passed the bottle to Dave. As soon as he tipped his head back to drink, the men stared directly at Laura. Unnerved, she redirected their gaze by pointing to the boy who was asleep. "Is that your son, Bruno?"

"No *señorita*, that Maria's boy, Paco."

Paco awoke at the sound of his name. He sat up and rubbed his eyes.

Dave passed the bottle back to Maria, then brought his thumb and index finger to his lips, as if smoking a joint. "Do you have any Bruno? I can pay."

"*Si señor*. I got sum good shit." He said something to his brothers in Spanish, then nodded for Dave to follow.

Laura's eyes bulged! She pulled Dave close and whispered, "WHERE DO YOU THINK YOU'RE GOING?"

"Did you forget why we came here?"

"Buy it here then—*right here*—don't leave me! Then we can go back to the condo like you promised."

"Don't get your panties in a knot! I'll be right back." He broke away from her grasp, then followed Bruno away from the fire. Lupe, who looked a few years younger than Bruno, followed Dave. They climbed over a hill, to the corner of a roughed in parking lot. There was no pavement beneath their feet, just dirt and the odd chunk of gravel. Lupe sat upon a boulder, in front of jungle brush yet to be cleared away.

"I'll take whatever fifty bucks will buy me." Dave handed American money to Bruno, who stuffed it into his pant pocket. "Aren't you going to count it?" Dave asked.

"Is okay *amigo*, you a good guy."

Lupe sat beside a knapsack that must have been stashed by the rock. He pulled a shotgun shell out of the bag and passed it to Dave. The shell was full of hemp. Bruno spoke Spanish to Lupe, who sparked a joint, the heater glowing bright red in the night. After a couple puffs, he passed it to Dave, who hauled on it like a newborn suckling!

"Look at *Mr. Bogart* go, eh Lupe?" The brothers broke into laughter.

Although Dave knew they were making fun of him for hogging the joint, he continued to toke until a coughing spell forced him to stop. He passed the joint to Bruno, who took a quick puff—then gave it right back to Dave! Dave suppressed the tail-end of his coughing spell, then embarked on a second round of vigorous smoking.

That was when he saw stars that were not of the night sky. The back of his head felt cleaved as he dropped to his knees. There was a clump of his hair and blood at the end of a tire iron, held by Lupe. In the instant between agony and nothingness, Dave panicked—*Laura!* He fell face first into the dirt. Bruno retrieved the shell packed with weed. Both brothers dashed back to the fire.

When they returned without Dave, Laura knew she was in trouble, turned and ran; but Lupe tackled her. The brothers held her down. She kicked and squirmed and screamed till Bruno punched her in the face. The father tied her hands behind her back while Lupe gagged her with a red bandana.

Paco watched in horror as his male kin carried Laura away. His mother and grandmother followed them in the moonlight; his great-grandmother was the only adult to stay behind.

As they lugged Laura past the far end of the parking lot, the father, who had hold of Laura's ankles, asked about "*gringo*." Bruno said, "Don't worry Papa: Lupe crack his big melon but *goood*!" Lupe smirked a thin, malicious grin.

But the brothers had underestimated the thickness of the *gringo's* skull. Lying facedown in the dirt, Dave murmured a groan. His head was throbbing…*and soaking wet*? Had it rained? No, he tasted saltwater on his lips. He sat up and wiped his face.

"*Urry, señor, urry, andale!*" It was the little boy, Paco. He hopped from foot to foot, shaking his emptied toy bucket. "*Com señor, urry, urry!*"

"Hold on kid! Let me think…where am I again?" A splitting headache sent waves of nausea down his spine. Then it hit him: *LAURA!* He stumbled to his feet. Paco tried to pull him into the parking lot, but Dave pushed him aside and tromped back to the fire, where he found the old woman sipping tequila. He glared at her: "*WHERE IS MY SISTER*?"

"Sorry *señor*, I no speak *Americano*." She stood and faced him.

"MY SISTER YOU IDIOT, *WHERE IS SHE*?"

Terrified, she glanced in the direction her boys had carried Laura. Dave failed to notice her involuntary signal. She held out the bottle. "You nice boy. Ave sum drink."

"I don't want a fucking drink! This is the last time I'm gonna ask—"

She took a two handed grip on the bottle and swung for his head! He grabbed her wrist and easily disarmed her. She looked into the darkness and screamed. Dave clued in: *She's trying to warn them I'm here.* He punched her in the mouth and her gums felt soft as rotten fruit. She fell to the sand and twitched.

With the tequila bottle in his hand, he ran in the direction she had telegraphed. He stopped in the middle of the parking lot about thirty meters from where he had been clubbed. As his eyes readjusted to the darkness, he saw the silhouettes of trees, boulders, mounds of dirt; nothing that looked like human activity. He listened intently: waves, a gentle breeze, a bus off in the distance—quick, laboured strides! He cocked the bottle back, ready to strike.

"*Señor, señor*!" It was Paco. Dave lowered the bottle. It made perfect sense to him now: *The boy didn't go back to the fire with me because he didn't want the old woman to know he was helping me.*

"Come *señor*, tis way!" Paco took off to the far end of the parking lot with Dave at his heels. They reached the top of a sandy ridge. Paco dropped to his stomach and pointed down the sand dune. "There *señor*, go, go—*andale*!"

A dim glow emanated from the closed curtains of a Volkswagen van. Dave ran to the front of the vehicle and peeked through the windshield. He saw Laura, gagged and bound. Her dress had been ripped open but her bra and panties were still in tact. Much of the van had been gutted. The men squatted around Laura on a steel floor, two brothers on each side of her, the father at the back holding her ankles. The mother was in the driver's seat, up on her knees watching them. Maria was on the passenger's seat, also on her knees watching.

As Dave chose his best angle of attack, the back or side door, Laura rammed her heel into the father's groin. While he keeled over in agony, the rest of the family broke into uproarious laughter!

Dave rolled the side door open. Their laughter subsided like trumpets gone breathless. Marco and Jose were on the far side of Laura; Bruno and Lupe were right in front of Dave, with their backs to him. Dave smashed the tequila bottle over Bruno's head and the neck of the bottle broke off in Dave's hand, a two inch shard sticking out the end. He grabbed Lupe by the hair and jammed the jagged glass into his throat.

"SON OF BITCH!" the father cried out. He tried to straighten up, but sharp spasms kept him doubled over.

Bruno had fallen forward, his greasy, grimy head lay on Laura's belly. She bucked her hips to get him off. Dave took a two handed grip of his ankle and flung him out of the vehicle. Meanwhile, Lupe had covered the gash on his throat with both hands. He staggered to stand, but toppled to the back of the van where his blood flooded the floor.

The mother pointed at the *gringo* and screamed Spanish at her two adolescent sons. All they did was cower like puppies accustomed to too many severe beatings. The father managed to straighten up. Still in obvious pain, he strained to reach a sawed-off shotgun, mounted on the ceiling above his head.

Meanwhile, Maria had extended herself over the passenger seat. She took a vicious swipe at Dave and scratched his cheek. But her outstretched position left her vulnerable. Dave grabbed her wrist, dragged her over the top of the seat, hauled her out of the van, and dropped her to the dirt. She rolled away from him, jumped to her feet and took off into the night.

By this time, the father had dropped a single shell into the shotgun. As he was closing the barrel, Laura kicked his hip—he buckled and the barrel snapped shut pointing up under his chin—the gun fired and a spray of buckshot blew his face off! He bounced off the wall and landed upon Lupe, father and son now corpses.

Dave cringed as the blast rang in his ears. The Mexican family—what was left of them—froze in horror. Marco glared at Laura: "YOU KILL MY PAPA!" He struggled to lift the edge of the mattress, but the weight of her made it awkward for him to get whatever he was going for. Dave punched him in the face. He would have given Jose a shot too, but the mother clawed at the *gringo's* eyes. Dave dealt her such a fierce backhand, she flew back into the dashboard and bounced her head off the windshield.

Meanwhile, Jose had helped his brother lift the mattress—Marco suddenly raised a hunting knife! Since the knife was out of Dave's reach, he pulled Jose across Laura, using him as a human shield. Marco checked up on his downward thrust, then jabbed at Dave, who took a quick step back, his right eye narrowly avoiding the point of the blade.

Maria charged out of the darkness, jumped upon his back and bit into his thick neck. He arched his spine and pulled her hair, but she held on like a leech. Marco lunged to stab the *gringo* but scraped his head against the top of the doorway, scalping a clump of hair off his head. The knife slipped out of his hand as he fell awkwardly contorted out of the van.

Dave spun around hard and smashed Maria into the passenger door. She slid off his back with a shriek.. As Marco grabbed the knife, Dave stepped on his wrist, disarmed him, then thrust the weapon between his shoulder blades. The mother opened the driver-side door and took off with Jose. Maria staggered to her feet and followed them.

Dave pulled the knife out of Marco and was about to chase the fleeing Mexicans, but stopped when he noticed Laura's eyes bulging out at him. He wiped the blade on Marco's shirt, then sliced through the bandana they had used to gag Laura.

"Don't you *dare* leave me again—*you big stupid idiot*!"

He cut the twine around her wrists and helped her out of the van. She held her torn dress together like a housecoat. They walked passed Bruno and Marco, both brothers laying gravely still. Nor did the old woman show any signs of life when they passed her near the red coals of the bonfire. The silhouette of a boy appeared upon the sand dune above his Great-grandma. Dave went to thank Paco but Laura grabbed his arm. "Where do you think you're going?"

"See the boy up there? If it wasn't for him—"

"Yes, if it wasn't for him, then what?"

"Never mind. Let's get back to the condo." He wanted to at least wave to the boy, but when he looked back, Paco was gone.

The stepsiblings walked along the beach in tortured contemplation. The tranquil harmony of waves and wind did little to ease their anguish. When they reached the lights of the first construction site, Laura said, "What do we do now, call the police?"

"Are you crazy? They'd lock me up and throw away the key! Not to mention the prisons here are *brutal* compared to the ones back home."

"So they'll get away with what they did to me?"

"Not really, Laura. I mean, most of those guys are dead!"

She started to sob.

"Don't worry Sis, everything will be alright."

"ALRIGHT? DO I LOOK ALRIGHT TO YOU?" She slapped his face.

Tears streamed down his cheek. "It was all my fault. I admit it…should never have taken you there."

She'd never seen him cry before, had thought he was incapable of it. "It wasn't all your fault. How were you supposed to know they were psycho? What happened when you left me at the fire?"

He explained how he'd been clubbed from behind and concluded with a teary eyed apology. She looked up at him in the moonlight and saw scratches on his cheek, as well as the bite mark on his neck. "You risked your life to save me. Thanks."

"We saved each other. If you hadn't kicked the father when he was loading the gun, he would have blown my head off—for sure!" An ambivalent mixture of terror and exhilaration filled their hearts.

When they reached the Paradise Beach Resort, Laura felt she could breathe again. They didn't want anyone to notice her torn dress, so she ducked into a cabana while he slinked amongst shadows, unobserved on his way to retrieve a change of clothes for her.

As anticipated, his parents were still out when he burst through the heavy oak door of their condo. He dashed to the medicine cabinet, downed four aspirins and cleaned himself up. Then he stuffed a bunch of Laura's things into a beach bag and returned to her at the cabana.

Laura bathed in the ocean, towelled off, then slipped into a grey sweat suit. Chilled, she sat in the cabana and leaned back into her brother. His bulky arms cuddled her cozy warm. "Know something Dave?"

"What's that?"

"Maybe *The Brady Bunch* wasn't so bad after all."

He held her until a bold, orange sun lit the ocean. While heading back to the condo, they prepared themselves for a reprimand but beat their parents home by twenty minutes.

Chapter One

Nearly a year later, November, 1978…As Miles Jarek Martini stood at his high school locker, he inhaled a musky perfume and it affected him like a puff of high-grade opium. Without looking, he knew Sheila Babcock had passed, heading for her nearby locker. Odds were it was Friday since Sheila skipped a lot of school, but never missed the last day of the week. He thought she was brilliant to attend Perth Bay High on her own terms, mostly on the cusp of a weekend.

Indeed, Monday and Tuesday mornings depressed Miles, especially that particular autumn, with its incessant grey skies and heavy morning frost, omens of an early winter in his home town of Kingston, Ontario. Amid the bleak weather, the lanky seventeen year old would pedal to school on his *Supercycle*, the cheap, heavy-as-lead bike, shaped like a ten speed racer but equipped with only three gears.

During his typical two kilometre clip to Perth Bay High, the wind would make his eyes water as the cold frosted his long brown hair, still damp from his morning shower. It made him look like he was crying while turning grey, as if going to school aged him prematurely. There wasn't much to brighten his day once he arrived. Besides excelling in Phys. Ed., he was a C+ student. He had but one true friend and that was through blood, a cousin who attended the same school.

So yes, he definitely envied Sheila Babcock's lofty schedule. Of course, she didn't miss every Monday and Tuesday; rather, she skipped school like a smooth stone across calm water, touching down every so often early in the week, always landing on Friday. Miles wondered how she got away with it. Wasn't there such a thing as truant officers? When you're built like Sheila Babcock, he reasoned, you could get away with just about anything! Not that he held it against her. The only thing he wanted to hold against her was himself.

His eyes, the color of robin's eggs, peeked passed his locker door to gaze at her, several meters down the hall. When he saw what she did to the boy next to her, Miles kicked the bottom of his locker.

Just then, Jo Martini approached. The stocky lad, with curly black hair and hazel eyes, stood with two textbooks and a heavily stuffed binder under his arm. He waited patiently for some sort of acknowledgement from his cousin.

"See that guy down there, by Sheila Babcock?" Miles said. "She just pinched his ass—for no apparent reason!"

"Yes, and good morning to you too, Miles."

"No, really. Every time I see her, she's giving some guy a hug, or putting an arm around someone or kissing some guy. They can't *all* be her boyfriends: don't think she even knows half the guys she does it to."

"Why does that bother you?"

"*I* never get any of that action. She never kisses me or pinches my ass."

"Don't know what you see in her."

"You mean besides her feathery blond hair? Besides her big, beautiful breasts? Besides her sexy ass in those tight jeans? Besides her—"

"*She certainly is more sexy than she is pretty.*"

"What's *that* supposed to mean?"

"Don't you think she's a little loose? I mean, is that what you'd want in a girlfriend?"

"Who said anything about a girlfriend?" Miles grabbed his geography books and closed his locker. "I'd do anything just to spend one night with her."

"*Anything?* I don't think so! Would you stick a needle in your eye?"

" Maybe not, but— "

"Would you drink a cup of raw sewage?"

"Not raw."

"Would you run head first into these lockers?"

"Yes, I'd definitely run headfirst into these lockers!" Miles dropped his books and stepped back several paces.

"Okay, Miles, you don't have to prove anything—I believe you!"

But Miles was already charging towards the steel doors. Jo let go of his books, then dropped his shoulder into his cousin, knocking him to the floor. It wasn't easy pinning Miles down. He was wiry but strong. Although they were fighting in jest, with intermittent bouts of laughter, each cousin was determined to get a leg up on the other.

A group of male teens chanted, "Fight, fight, fight!" A young woman stepped around them and said, "Why don't you guys grow up!"

"*Grow up*?" Miles said, with the side of his face pressed against the carpet, "How's this for grown up?" He threw himself into a series of violent, bucking convulsions.

Jo pushed his feet against the carpet, leveraging his chest against Miles's back, keeping him pinned face down. His extra twelve pounds always came in handy whenever they wrestled like this. Frustrated, Miles no longer struggled in jest. The violence of his contortions escalated till his head snapped back and split his cousin's lip. "Uh, sorry about that Jo—you alright?"

Jo didn't respond; instead, he slipped Miles into a full nelson! "Aha—the only way you'll get out of this hold is to gnaw one of your own arms off!"

Miles didn't take his word for it. He flailed like a madman in a straightjacket. After burning off most of the caloric intake from his breakfast, he managed to struggle himself into submission! Between panting breaths, he said, "*LET—ME—GO*!"

"Alright," Jo said, "I get it. You're crazy about her. If I let you go, do you promise you won't run into the lockers?"

Miles thought for a moment, then said, "What a ridiculous thing to have to promise!"

As they broke up in laughter, Jo released Miles and the crowd dispersed. Panting, the two cousins got to their feet. Miles leaned back against a locker and raked his fingers through his long brown hair. Jo bent over and caught his breath while resting his hands upon his knees.

Miles's heartbeat was almost back to normal when he inhaled a whiff of Sheila's potent perfume. She said to Jo, "Nice butt!" and patted him there, *twice*. To Miles, it seemed to unfold in slow motion, her hand swinging back, then forward onto Jo's butt cheek. Did she cop a feel in there, or did Miles just imagine her long, red fingernails sinking into his flesh?

Jo stammered a "thank-you" to Sheila, then watched her walk away, clearly entranced by the rhythmic sway of her hips.

"What an ass!" Miles said, as he snatched his books off the floor.

"I have to admit," Jo said, "she *is* voluptuous—Oh, you meant *I'm* an ass. You're mad at me? Come on, I didn't do anything. I don't even like her! Hey, wait up! I have to fix my binder, the darn thing exploded on me."

Miles stomped off down the hallway.

Jo called down to him, "I'll meet you for lunch. I'm buying, OKAY?"

***

Though the stately, well-travelled geography teacher described the terrains of Tunguska with great enthusiasm, Miles didn't hear a word she said. As if he could think of anything other than the Sensual Goddess who had just touched his cousin's ass—*twice*! When he heard the word *permafrost*, however, it struck a chord in him because he felt it in his heart.

By lunchtime, his animosity towards Jo had dissipated. After all, Sheila had approached him from behind; Jo didn't even see her coming. Miles thought, what claim do I have on her anyway? She doesn't even know I exist! Friday's special was cheeseburger and fries. Miles was starving. Didn't Jo say he was buying?

The cafeteria at Perth Bay High doubled as an auditorium, with a stage at the front and a balcony at the back. Jo stood with his cousin in a long line-up leading to the kitchen. "Here Miles, take my knapsack and find us a couple of seats."

Miles slid the strap over his shoulder. "What do you have in here? *Bricks*?"

"Yes, bricks of knowledge. You might have heard of them, they're called books."

Miles rolled his eyes, then bumped and pushed his way into the crowd. What a chaotic zoo! He turned sideways and slipped between yammering peers. Along the middle aisle, he dodged past two male students and claimed the last two available seats.

The instant he sat upon the beige, plastic chair, he thought, wait a minute, those two guys I just cut in front of: cowboy boots, leather football jackets—*what have I done?*

Dave Needler grabbed Miles by his shirt collar and held him up, heavy knapsack and all. "Whoa now little doggie, where do you think you're goin'?"

Miles squirmed to free himself, but one of the other guys gave him a stiff kick between the buttocks. He cringed as the pointy toe of the boot sent a shock wave of pain through his anus. He caught his breath and said, "Why don't you guys sit here?"

"Mighty generous of you," Dave said, then shoved him back into the crowd.

Miles caromed off a couple students, then bumped into the back of Dave's stepsister. A friend of hers, who stood before her, caught Laura as she stumbled forward. He meant to apologize, but when Laura glared at him, with eyes dark as black pearls, her beauty left him speechless—absolutely stunning how her sheen black hair fell over her shoulders and draped upon her icy-blue, cashmere sweater.

She didn't take pity on him when it became obvious her beauty had tied his tongue. "Watch where you're going—*jerk*!"

"Sorry, I…I was pushed." He smiled and hoped to win her over with his best puppy-dog look. But her eyes didn't soften and the other girls joined her in staring him down. "Okay, you got me," he said, "I get a big thrill out of bumping into people!"

He pulled the strap of Jo's knapsack back over his shoulder and wandered along the front row of tables. He started to look for a place to sit on the floor when a couple of students vacated an end table. Miles rushed over, dropped the heavy knapsack on one chair and sat on the other.

All the hollering and laughter melded into a continuous roar. A chocolate chip cookie spiralled through the air and dinged Miles on his cheek. He barely flinched. He was too busy scoping the room for Sheila.

If Miles had had a tail, it would have been wagging when Jo set down a tray heaped with two cheeseburgers, french-fries and two large cartons of chocolate milk. Half way through his meal, Jo said, "So where's Sheila sitting?"

"Back right corner, under the balcony."

"Ever wonder if any of the rumours about her are true?"

"Don't tell me you believe any of that garbage!"

"One thing's for certain: her father's doing time in the Perth Bay Pen. I read about it in the newspaper."

"So! We live in Kingston, Ontario the incarceration capital of Canada! With seven pens in the area there are more inmates around here than anywhere else in the country. It's just a matter of odds we'd know someone who had a family member doing time. Does that make Sheila a bad person?"

"What about the witchcraft? Her mother's known to be a priestess in the occult. Rumour has it, teachers from this very school attend Sheila's house for séances and other rituals of black magic."

Miles broke into such a spasm of laughter, chocolate milk nearly came out his nose! After clearing his windpipe, he said, "Don't tell me you believe in witches! How about vampires? Maybe she's the *Daughter of Dracula!* Or how about monsters? Haven't you heard? Sheila's the *Bride of Frankenstein*!"

"Don't laugh, Miles. I read in *McLean's* magazine, there are about twenty thousand practicing witches in Canada and three times that many in the States."

"Hey Jo, do you believe everything you read? And anyway, even if her family is into witchcraft, everyone has to have *something* to believe in."

"Okay Miles, what about her sister? I heard Sheila has a sister who was recently released from an asylum."

Miles really got his back up this time. "Just because her sister might be crazy doesn't mean Sheila is. Besides, my own mother sees a psychiatrist and you're nice to her."

"Good point, Pal. I was out of line there, sorry." Jo had to wonder though, Hadn't his cousin learned anything living with a mother who popped mild tranquilizers like they were breath mints? He had seen aunt Betty come undone over the years, crying one moment, screaming the next. It wasn't pretty. Why would Miles want to increase his exposure to erratic mood swings and emotional turmoil, likely manifest in Sheila's family?

"Anyway," Miles said, "I'd definitely put up with a little craziness if that's what it took to feel her wicked body next to mine!"

"Know something Coz, there's more to women than their 'wicked bodies.'"

Miles gave Jo a suspicious glare. "You're not gay, right? Just refined?"

"Very funny. I just think you could do better than Sheila. She seems like nothing but trouble."

Miles swallowed his last bite of burger and washed it down with a big gulp of chocolate milk. "If you're so high and mighty, who's your idea of the perfect girl?"

"Sorry, that's classified."

"Come on, tell me who you like."

"I'll give you a hint: Her hair flows like thick, black silk, in the wake of her regal walk. Her eyes glow like halos, reflecting a deep, mysterious beauty. Her smile radiates like a thousand suns. Her— "

"Jeepers creepers, Jo! Where do you come up with this stuff? From some novel you read, right? Just tell me who she is!"

"I love to read. It's not a crime."

"Nobody's perfect, I guess. Just tell me who you like without all the hoopla."

"I'll tell you her name if she agrees to go out with me. Until then, *discretion's the better part of valour*."

Miles raised his eyes and sighed.

Jo pulled a thick book out of his knapsack. "Speaking of novels, here's one I think you'd enjoy. It's called *Don Quioxte.* It's full of action, humour, and the way he praises women, well my friend, you could learn a thing or two!"

Miles took the novel and slammed it on the table. "You and your books! You can't live your life out of some book. You've got to get out there and experience the world firsthand."

"Why can't you do both? Develop yourself through reading and by living in the real world?"

Miles had his eyes locked on Sheila Babcock. Her legs were crossed and her foot was extended beyond the table. She dangled a red, high heeled shoe on the end of her toe. Three of her guy friends suddenly stood up and climbed the balcony stairs. They were scruffy, long haired fellows in black leather vests. Sheila stepped into her shoe and followed them up the stairs.

"I can get *artsy fartsy* without reading some book," Miles said. "I went out for dinner with my parents last week and my mom ordered *Strawberry Flambé*. Sheila is like Strawberry Flambé because it's made with strawberries and Sheila's hair is strawberry blond. Flambé is set on fire and Sheila is definitely hot! It's alcohol that makes the dessert flammable and I feel light-headed whenever I see her, like I've been drinking. Flambé is creamy and rich, like her thick, luscious lips!"

"Not bad Miles, great analogy. Based on how crazy you are about Sheila, I think you'd relate to Don Quixote. He's in love with Dulcinea, whose beauty he says is peerless and superhuman; her status, at least that of a princess. In reality, she's a peasant he once saw in passing but likely never met. In other words, he's infatuated with a woman he barely knows! Sound familiar?"

"Uh-huh," Miles murmured, as he watched Sheila step down the balcony stairs.

Jo crossed his arms and said, "The burger you just ate was full of maggots."

"Hm, really eh?"

"The price of beans went up in China."

"Right on Jo. Hey, something's up with Sheila. Looks like she's crying."

"I knew you weren't listening!"

"I'm gonna take a closer look." Miles moseyed to the back of the caff, dropped upon one knee, untied his shoe, retied it, stood up slowly, then returned to his seat.

Jo sighed. "Well?"

"Strange. First she was sobbing, I mean tears were streaming down her cheek. Then she burst into laughter!"

Jo shook his head. "Not that she's crazy or anything."

"Maybe I'll see her at the dance tonight. What time are you picking me up?"

"Sorry Miles, can't make it."

"*What are you talking about*?"

"I'm working on a special project."

"You're doing homework on Friday night? Take a break, man! Let's get a mickey of lemon gin and check out the action at the dance."

"First of all, I don't drink that gut rot. Second of all, the project isn't for school. It's for….well, all I can say is that I'll be busy this whole weekend."

"Wait a minute! This has to do with your mystery girl, doesn't it? What's your plan? Gonna swim across Lake Ontario to prove your undying love?"

"*Very Funny*!"

"So I have to fly solo tonight? Alright, guess I can handle it. At least I'll have something decent to wear. I'm meeting my mother at the mall to buy a new shirt."

"Have fun at the dance. Sorry I can't make it; but hopefully, I'll have some huge news for you on Monday or Tuesday. Until then, take care."

Miles thanked his cousin for lunch. On his way to history class, he tried to guess who Jo's mystery girl might be. Whoever she is, he thought, she must be pretty special, *like the frickin' Queen of Sheba*!

***

After school, Miles caught a bus and met his mother, Betty, at the mall. The stout, red headed woman sat on a bench, eating the final square of a large chocolate bar. "MILES!" she said, apparently ecstatic to see him. "I bought this chocolate bar for us to share but got carried away. Do you want one of your own?"

"No thanks. Let's get shopping."

"You're speakin' my language Son: Let's shop till we drop!"

She hustled him past the cool stores like Bootlegger and Thrifty's, then pulled him downstairs into Bargain Barney's Basement Warehouse. The septic scent down there made him breathe through his mouth. After hunting through racks and racks of discount clothing, Miles found a navy-blue shirt that didn't make him cringe. He tried on a size medium but the sleeves were three inches too short. He tried on a large. It covered his arms alright but was way too puffy in the chest.

Meanwhile, Betty had been conducting her own search. She handed him her idea of a perfect shirt, which was to say a perfect bargain. As soon as he saw the dizzy, red-checkered shirt, Miles hated it! And he hated it more when he tried it on. The material felt scratchy, like wax paper. "Mom, I'm not fussy on the material. Plus, it's too big."

"You'll grow into it and there's nothing wrong with the material!"

"Yeah, if you like wearing a plastic tablecloth!"

"MILES—this is a great shirt, at a great price!"

"MOM—there's a reason why it's so cheap!"

"Let's get to the register before there's a line-up."

Before long, Miles was sitting on the bus with his mother. She held an ice-cream cone in one hand, and in the other, a Barney's merchandise bag that boasted, *Another satisfied customer!*

Later, when he was in his room, he dropped "*scratchy shirt*" onto the floor and kicked it under his bed. He rummaged through his drawers to find an alternative. Pants weren't a problem: his grandmother had sent him a pair of TEK jeans from Slovenia. The rare brand of denim, made in China, happened to fit him perfectly.

Perhaps a simple T-shirt would do the trick. A sort of Fonzie look. No. Wearing a T-shirt in November would make him look poor. He liked a tartan, flannel shirt his aunt had given him last Christmas; but, as usual, the sleeves were too short. He pulled it on anyway. The tapered waist seemed to broaden his shoulders. He rolled the cuffs back one turn. Perfect—for all he knew, three quarter sleeves were in style!

But when his mother saw him, she asked why he wasn't wearing his new shirt.

"I've decided to save it for a special day at school."

"Nonsense! The whole reason we shopped today was to buy you a shirt for the dance. NOW GO PUT IT ON!" Clearly, he had little choice but to obey.

Miles buttoned his jean jacket up to his chin, thereby hiding every bit of his new shirt. He then stormed out of the house, hopped on a bus and sat alone on the back bench. His arms were crossed, his ankles were crossed—he was cross! He certainly wouldn't be seen at the dance wearing scratchy shirt. He only knew one sure-fire way of easing his humiliation: booze. He got off the bus and entered a liquor store.

Alone in an aisle, he opened a couple buttons of his jacket, snatched a mickey of lemon gin, slipped it into his baggy shirt, then headed for the exit. As he neared the checkout, a short, grey-haired man stepped in front of him. "Can I help you, son?"

The lanky teen froze. His heart pounded in his throat. "I'll be eighteen in three months. Is that close enough to buy something here or do I have to wait?"

The intricate maze of wrinkles about the old man's face softened into a sympathetic grin. "You definitely have to wait, son."

"Oh. Ok. Guess I'll come back then, then." He scampered out of the store.

Now he really needed a drink. He headed north passed the city limits, then took refuge along a meandering path into a forest. The lemon gin was easy to drink straight, didn't take him long to get a good buzz going. This is better than going to the dance, he thought. As for Sheila Babcock, well, she was just a pipe-dream, wasn't she? He suddenly stopped and looked up. "Besides, there's not a girl on Earth who can match the beauty of *that* tree, right there!"

The giant maple tree towered above him upon a cliff. Autumn had already claimed its leaves. Moonlight glimmered from its silvery branches. "The view from the top of that tree must be spectacular!" he said.

After Miles slipped the bottle back in his shirt, he scaled a slope beside the cliff, then pulled himself into the tree. He climbed until the branches he clung to swayed in the gusty wind. Whoa! he thought, this is high enough.

He wedged his running shoe in the middle of a Y-shaped branch and hooked his arm around one of the offshoots. He swallowed a belt of gin and looked around. The view up there was indeed spectacular! To his left, city lights mimicked the stars above; to his right, imposing limestone walls towered around the Perth Bay Pen.

Climbing three stories of maple bolstered his alcoholic rush. His cheeks were flush and toasty. He would have enjoyed complete euphoria except scratchy shirt had chafed his nipples, tender and sore!

Miles slipped the mickey into his pants and hung his jacket upon a branch. As he yanked open the front of his shirt, buttons popped off and rained upon the forest floor. He then pulled the ill-fitting eyesore off his back, rolled it into a ball and tossed it out of the tree. A gust of wind puffed it open and carried it towards the moon, like a tacky, red-chequered balloon!

As the crisp November air soothed his bare nipples, he watched a bus pull into the pen. He felt akin to the inmates because, like him, they suffered one lonely night after another, without the touch of a woman. But convicts deserved it: they were being punished! Miles wondered what crimes he had committed to be so all alone.

A chill ran up his spine and goose bumps covered him from head to toe. He slipped back into his jacket and swallowed a belt of gin. The tree rocked him like a cradle. He cringed when he thought about his lack of friends. Other than Jo, his only companions were a group of regulars he knew from an outdoor basketball court. "Where's Jo when you need him?" Miles lamented. But then he thought, Jo doesn't have to hold my hand whenever I go out!

No matter what he told himself, Miles missed his cousin. His shoulders slumped forward. His chin sunk to his chest. The branches below seemed like a downward spiral. What if I never find a girl who likes me? What if I die a virgin? He furrowed his brows: *Stop feeling sorry for yourself—ya WIMP*!

He gulped down what was left of the mickey and tossed the bottle out of the tree. It fell over the cliff, then exploded upon rocks. Brimming with Dutch courage, he shimmied up to where branches were so thin, he could whiplash himself to and fro. He tossed his head back and howled at the moon!

Then, razor sharp panic—his fingers, numb from the cold, lost their grip! Down, down, down—he flailed and groped while the tree battered him like a gauntlet of paddle whacks. He twisted and reached to catch himself, but a branch bashed his forehead. His limp body then flopped through the tree like a raggedy doll. His mother must have told him a thousand times that he would fall and break his neck. And now… "POOF!" He landed flat on his back, upon a pocket of leaves. The tree had spit him out a meter from the edge of the cliff.

When he came to, his body felt numb. He lifted his watch to the moonlight: It read 10:05, but the face was cracked and the second hand wasn't moving. He climbed down the cliff and stagger-jogged out of the forest.

The buses were no longer running, which meant it was past midnight. It took Miles three hours to walk home. As soon as he stepped inside, Betty accosted him with her hand raised, ready to strike; but then she noticed cuts and scrapes on his face. "What in God's name happened to you?"

"Some guys jumped me after the dance. They tore my new shirt to pieces."

"What's that smell on your breath? You been drinking?"

He stared at the floor.

"Well, serves you right then! Your father worked a double shift today so I won't wake him—lucky for you—now get to bed before I….Just go to bed!"

He was half way to his room when she called out to him, "Hold on. Better let me put something on those scrapes, or they might get infected."

***

It seemed to Miles like he'd just fallen asleep when the vacuum cleaner slammed into his headboard: "BANG, BANG, VARUMMM, BANG, BANG…"

He awoke with a jolt. "WHAT—WHAT IS IT?"

"RISE AND SHINE SUNSHINE—TIME TO FACE THE MUSIC!"

Once Miles realized that it wasn't a freight train coming through his room, that it was just his pain-in-the-ass mother, he buried his head under the pillow. After Betty vacuumed his room—more thoroughly than usual—she yanked the pillow off his head. "YOUR FATHER WANTS TO SPEAK TO YOU!"

"WHY DON'T YOU SHUT THAT THING OFF SO YOU DON'T HAVE TO YELL?"

Defiant, she strolled out of his room with the vacuum roaring in tow.

Miles wanted to face the music, wanted get it over with. But first, he made a mad dash to the washroom, where he puked his guts out. Every muscle in his body ached and his ribs cramped with a stabbing pain whenever he inhaled. As nausea pressed beads of sweat out his forehead, he made a deal with God that he would *never* drink again.

He brushed his teeth, then hobbled to the kitchen table. When Betty greeted him with runny eggs and sausages, Miles had to look away. His tongue felt like thistles and burrs. He took two sips of orange juice, then downed it all.

Anton Martini sat at the table, cloaked behind his morning paper. The forty-two-year-old father was shorter and less willowy than his son, but in decent shape due to physical labour at a textile plant. He lowered the corner of his paper. "You know Miles, you upset your mother last night when you came home so late."

"Sorry dad, it won't happen again."

"I also heard you were drinking."

"Believe me, the way I feel right now, I'll never touch the stuff again!"

"You do look pale. I suppose that's punishment enough this time. No more alcohol, though, not until you're of age. Do I make myself clear?"

"Crystal clear, dad. May I go back to bed?"

"Before you go, tell me something: Who beat you up?"

"These guys in ski masks—"

"*Ski masks*, eh?" his father interrupted, "You don't want to be a snitch. I can respect that. Next time, be more careful. As for today, you're grounded. I want you to stay home and think about what you did. Understand?"

"Yes, sir."

"You're excused from the table."

After Miles left, Betty laid into Anton for being too lenient. "We were that age once," he said, "remember our prom night?" As Betty blushed, Anton shook his paper and turned the page.

***

Even after sleeping half the day away, Miles still felt woozy. He walked gingerly to the kitchen and poured himself a glass of ginger ale. Much to his relief, his parents were out shopping. He turned on the TV, flopped upon the couch and watched a rerun of *Star Trek,* the episode where….

A power surge in the transporter sends Captain Kirk, Scotty, Lieutenant Uhura and Dr. McCoy, into a parallel universe. Most everything's the same, except this version of the *Enterprise* is crewed by lewd savages, part of an evil empire!

In this alternate reality, Kirk is shocked to find he has a sultry, exotic concubine, "The Captain's Girl," waiting for him in his quarters. Inevitably, he seizes her in his arms and plasters an open-mouthed kiss upon her lips. *Kirk never had it so good on his own ship*! Miles thought.

Shortly thereafter, Lieutenant Uhura saunters up to "evil" Sulus, the lusty, bloodthirsty alter-ego of the mild-mannered officer she knows back home. Part of an intricate plan to return the landing party to its proper universe, she distracts him from his monitors by flaunting her voluptuous body all over him.

That's it! Miles said to himself. He marched to his bedroom and pulled a dated issue of *Penthouse* magazine out from under his mattress. A few minutes later, he basked in the afterglow of an intense, spasmodic release. As he fell asleep, he wondered if there were real girls out there like those insatiable models in *Penthouse*, who wore racy lingerie and craved sex as much as a guy. Only in my dreams, he thought, only in my dreams…

***

At five o'clock, his mother roused him for dinner. He felt much better, although a moderate degree of stiffness lingered in his ribs and neck. Betty served him green beans, potatoes and meatloaf. "Umm," he said, "This tastes great!"

Anton raised his eyebrows. His mother said, "It's only meatloaf."

"Yeah, but it's the best you've ever made!"

After two and a half helpings, Miles was stuffed. A couple of hours later, he tried to watch the hockey game with his father, but fell asleep during the first period.

***

The next morning Miles awoke, bursting with energy. He had never felt more rested in his entire life! After a hearty bacon and egg breakfast, the spry teen bolted outside to play basketball. He dribbled six blocks to an outdoor court, which was vacant as a ghost town, apparently too cold for anyone else to play. Indeed, he had bundled up in long johns, a turtle neck, a sweat suit, and a heavy wool sweater. Still, he was chilled to the bone. A hole in the toe of his running shoe allowed cold air to seep in around his foot.

But he knew all about raw hustle and the *great internal furnace*. He practiced the stutter step. He shoulder faked left, then tore off to the right. He dribbled full speed, pulled up for a jump shot, raced to the net, then snared the rebound before the ball hit the ground. He dribbled around and between his legs in a figure eight, then tore off to the other end of the court and fired another shot.

Twelve minutes of dodging about the court thawed his sinews. The feeling came back in his fingers. His cheeks were toasty and rosy red. He whipped off his sweater and tossed it to the sidelines. Since the wind blew his shots towards the south, he aimed to the north side of whichever net he was shooting at. He was accustomed to making such adjustments. He never had enough confidence to try out for the school team and played almost exclusively outdoors. The odd shot rattled around the rim and fell in.

Eventually, Miles stripped down to his T-shirt and sweatpants. The Arctic air mass now refreshed him, saved him from overheating. Suddenly hot, he made one shot after another, leading to the feeling he could not miss! He closed his eyes and fired a twenty footer—SWISH! He pumped his fist back and forth and broke into manic laughter. *Perhaps I should try out for the school team,* he thought.

He went on a dribbling spree, pulled up twenty feet from a hoop, then said to himself, *If I make this shot, I'll introduce myself to Sheila Babcock.* He fired five degrees to the north side of the basket—SWISH!

He seized the ball and dribbled to the top of the key at the other end of the court. *If this one goes in, I'll ask her out to a movie.* As soon as the ball left his finger tips, he knew the shot was binding—SWISH!

Miles sprinted to the hoop, latched onto the ball, dribbled down the court and pulled up twenty-five feet from the basket. "*If I make this next shot,*" he said out loud, "*I'll kiss her on the lips and slip her my tongue*!"

He took a deep breath and on the exhale, released the shot. Perfect follow-through, soaring arch....but he had overpowered it by a fraction—the ball hit the back of the rim and bounced right out again. "Damn it!" he said. All bets were off. He wouldn't introduce himself to Sheila Babcock, wouldn't ask her out, and he certainly wouldn't be kissing her with a bold tongue! *Who am I kidding?* He thought. *She's way out of my league. Just shoot the ball and forget about her!*

Three boys in snowsuits moseyed up to the court. After Miles drained three consecutive baskets, one of the youngsters asked, "Who do you play for?"

"Well, nobody," Miles said.

The boy raised his eyebrows in disbelief. Miles was tired of being a nobody. He pictured himself nailing those baskets in a gym full of cheering students. Tryouts for the Perth Bay Pikes were to be held in two days. Since this was his last year of high school, it would be his one and only chance to make the team.

***

That night at the dinner table, Miles waited patiently to speak. What was Betty going on about this time? Curtains. She wanted new curtains, but Anton wouldn't relinquish funds to her. When she paused to release a consternated sigh, Miles cut in: "You guys should have seen me shoot baskets today!"

"Miles, your father is colorblind. The turquoise curtains obviously clash with my burgundy sofa. You can see that, right?"

"*I don't know, mom*. Dad, you played basketball in high school, didn't you?"

"A little." Anton wasn't usually disinterested in his son. But on that particular evening, his priority was to curb Betty's spending frenzy. He worked hard and hated living paycheque to paycheque. "We didn't need a new sofa but you bought one anyway," he said to his wife, "Now you're carping about curtains? If they don't match, *dye them*!"

Miles jumped in again: "One of my running shoes has a hole in the toe. Could I buy a new pair before I try out for the basketball team on Tuesday morning?"

His parents gave him *squint eye* and lectured him on the money tree they didn't have, on how lucky he was compared to kids starving in Ethiopia and Bangladesh. Clearly, the shoe issue didn't have a leg to stand on!

Miles gave up on his parents. While twirling spaghetti with his fork, he breathed deeper and deeper, until he was firing jump shots in a gym full of cheering peers. Of course, a particular blond bombshell sat in the stands, donning a tight T-shirt with the team's mascot, a sharp-toothed Pike, stretched across her bountiful breasts.

Whereas Anton relished the silent treatment phase of their arguments, Betty hated it. While choking on resentment, she picked up her dishcloth and fired it at Miles— SPLAT! His face was plastered with stinking dankness.

"*Whatchya do that for, mom*?"

"Earth to Miles, Earth to Miles, come in please!"

He used his sleeve to wipe the damp stench off his face, then excused himself from the table, happy to escape his ill-tempered parents.

***

On Monday night, the eve before the tryout, Miles lay in his bed wide-awake. He hated going to bed when he wasn't tired, but Betty enforced a ridiculous bedtime at nine o'clock. Sheila and basketball; basketball and Sheila: it was all he could think about. He counted headlights that flashed across his wall every time a car turned onto his street. By the time his parents went to bed, Miles had counted sixty-seven cars. An hour later, it was dead quiet and pitch dark. He resigned himself to the possibility he'd be awake all night, then promptly fell asleep. Even then, he failed to relax, awoken twice by the jolt of his legs running horizontal sprints beneath his blankets… ZZZ…

Emerging from the darkness of his closet, Sheila Babcock wore nothing but a Perth Bay bodysuit, the type the girls wore in gym class, only the school's mascot, a sharp-toothed pike, looked more like a brawny barracuda. He sat up on the edge of his bed, wearing nothing but his skivvies; she stepped between his legs and nestled his face against her sexy, cozy bosom...

When his alarm blared at six, remnants of her racy embrace held him spellbound. He shut off his alarm and lingered in her rapture…*nearly fell back asleep*—then jumped out of bed, bursting with nervous energy. He rushed through his morning routine, headed to the front door and was about to step into his raggedy runners but noticed a rectangular box with "Converse" on the lid! A short note was attached:

"*Dear Miles,*
Sorry I can't give you a lift this morning, but I'm working another double shift (have to pay for those darn curtains, eh?). A friend from the plant has an uncle who owns Alfred's Sporting Goods. He was kind enough to meet me after closing, said that Converse made the best basketball shoes. Good Luck with your tryout!
Love, Dad."

Miles opened the box to find a pair of white-canvas low-tops, the ones with a red racing stripe around each shoe. Thrilled, the lanky teen laced up his new dekes, bolted outside, jumped on his bike and clipped through the crisp morning air. As wind made his eyes water, he couldn't remember a time when he loved his dad more.

***

Miles sat in the change room, not knowing where to look. His mouth was dry, his tongue shackled. Since he failed to join a conversation, he felt more akin to the clothing hooks on the wall than to any of the other players.

Upon shaky knees, he entered the gym. As part of an open-concept design, a spectators' window on the second floor overlooked the court from above the west-end backboard. The bird's eye view had always been his favourite place to watch games. Normally, Miles loved to be in the gym, but this morning he felt sick to his stomach. His eyes were wide as delft blue saucers. His heart pounded like an erratic drum. *What am I doing here*? he thought. He looked up at the spectators' window: *that's where I belong!*

A whistle blew and the coach organized a scrimmage. Miles dragged himself up and down the court, as if trapped in a nightmare. He perceived reality. Still framed. One snapshot. At a time. The logical flow. Of the game. Eluded him. Completely. In such a disoriented state, the thought of touching the ball terrified him. On offence, he hid behind other players so that he was never open for a pass. On defence, opponents blew by him like he was standing still because he was, in fact, standing still a lot, a perfect mannequin for his new shoes.

After a while, nobody bothered to cover him. Then, a teammate dribbled in the offensive zone and was trapped by two veteran players. Out of sheer desperation, he bounced a pass to Miles, who suddenly found himself standing with the ball, wide open, ten feet from the net. He got rid of the ball as if it were a hot potato, chucking it towards the basket, but well short of the rim. "*NICE AIR BALL*!" somebody shouted. Several players snickered.

During a brief stoppage in play, he thought, *I'll be the first one cut!* He closed his eyes, tilted his head back and sighed. When he opened his eyes again, he saw someone above the backboard, watching from the spectators' window. He could have sworn it was Sheila Babcock but couldn't be sure from that far away.

The scrimmage resumed as a skinny, long-haired kid started to dribble out of his own end. Miles leapt in front of him and shuffled his new Converse shoes violently across the hardwood floor, funnelling the kid to the side of the court. The dribbler pulled up before he was run out of bounds! He found himself trapped between Miles and the sidelines. The instant he looked for someone to pass to, Miles stripped him of the ball. "*Friggin' hack*!" the kid yelled out.

As Miles dribbled full tilt down the court, Hank Reddick, a starter from last year's squad, scrambled back to cover him. But Miles grounded to a halt and skied himself for a jump shot: straight right elbow, fluid release, plenty of arc—SWISH!

Making the basket fuelled him with manic energy. As soon as the ball was in play again, he embarked on a one man, full-court press, leaping from one opponent to another, convulsing at them like he was having upright, epileptic seizures—rushing and confusing ball handlers, thrown off guard by his whirlwind tenacity.

Miles eventually relented and melded into the other players. Relieved, his opponent tossed a pass across the court. As the ball left his finger tips, Miles tore off to intercept it! After snatching the ball out of the air, he dribbled full tilt down the court, pulled up at the top of the key and fired his second jumper: straight right elbow, plenty of arc—but he had put too much on it, the ball hit the back of the rim and bounced right out again.

The coach blew a whistle and thanked everyone for coming out. Miles looked for Sheila above the backboard, but the window cell was empty. I must have been seeing things, he thought, That's okay, I just gave myself a chance at making the team!

He rushed his shower, wrapped a towel around his waist, then dashed out into the hallway. He found the freshly posted roster sheet and when he saw his name at the bottom of the list, he jumped around the hall, pumping his fist back and forth, chanting, "YES, YES, YES!" Amid his jubilation, the towel slipped off his hips, just as an Asian girl from his geography class happened by. Startled by his wet rat, she picked up her pace considerably! Unfazed, Miles scooped his towel off the floor and darted back into the change room.

When he rejoined his new teammates, three of the popular players, Hank Reddick, Art Hornbeak and Tate Cooke, were discussing pro football. Miles burst into their conversation: "Hey guys, I made the team!"

They stared at him. Hank Reddick said, "Oh." They then resumed their discussion, ignoring him completely.

Miles left the change room wondering if it was such a great thing he had made the team after all. When he reached his locker, he struggled to remember his combination. It wasn't even 9 o'clock yet and he was exhausted. The numbers were scrambled in his head. Was it 24-34-36? No, that didn't work. He tried 34-24-36. That wasn't it either. Finally, he turned the dial, 36-24-34 and the tumblers relented.

He opened the door, only to have his books fall to the floor. After he dropped upon bended knee, red polished toenails appeared, sheathed in sheer pantyhose, peeking at him through the peepholes of black, high heeled shoes.

Already aware of who stood there, he peered passed her frayed denim skirt, beyond her buoyant, braless bust-line, to her tantalizing smile, alluring enough to bend time. As she wished him a good morning, her fawning brown eyes beamed the warmth of sunshine.

His thoughts cut through her spellbinding sensuality: *SPEAK!* he told himself. "Hi. Sheila. Good morning." So close was she, the scent of her Opium perfume made his head swim. A critical voice shouted in his head: *STOP BEING A BOAR—STAND UP AND INTRODUCE YOURSELF!*

He managed to stand up alright, but Sheila deemed a verbal introduction unnecessary; the instant he was on his feet, she planted a brief but potent kiss upon his lips. *Shoot first, ask questions later* must have been her motto. When their eyes met, she said, "I watched you play basketball this morning, you were amazing!"

"I was?"

"Oh, and modest too! What happened at the end? You really caught on fire!"

"Come to think of it, I played better after I saw you up in the window. Guess you inspired me."

"Aw, that's sweet." She planted another kiss upon his lips. "Would you like to walk me home after school today?"

"*Would I!* I mean, yeah, that'd be great."

"I'll meet you at the main entrance." She kissed him once more, as if doing so were already standard procedure. As he watched the sway of her hips merge into the crowd, he wondered, did that really just happen, or did I dream it?

He restored order to his locker, then bolted off to math class where his teacher, a crusty old man with pasty, horseshoe baldness, blasted him for being tardy. Miles didn't bother explaining that the girl of his dreams had just kissed him—*three times*—and so he didn't give a damn about being late!

The lecture, on the significance of pi, penetrated his mind like wind against a steel dome! He recollected, over and over again, every minute detail of his first intimate encounter with Sheila and couldn't wait to see her again. The clock on the wall seemed to move slower every minute, as if drying in cement. Resigned to doing time in class, he leaned back in his chair, locked his fingers behind his head and thought about a quote his well-read cousin once mentioned: *Careful what you wish for—you just might get it!*

He didn't understand what Jo had meant at the time; but now Miles wondered how many more wishes would come true with the girl of his just met dreams.

Chapter Two

Miles wasn't the only Martini teen enamoured on that Tuesday morning in November. His cousin Jo slipped out of biology class five minutes early, en route to divulge his love to Laura Needler.

Though they had never met during their first years of high school, Genghis Khan brought them together for a group project, during their grade thirteen history class. While they discussed the Mongrel warrior's dogged determination to break through The Great Wall of China, Laura's enigmatic beauty smote Jo like a thousand arrows! Like most everyone, he was wowed by her spectacular, sheen black hair. But what really enthralled him was her passionate eyes, emboldened by irises that were nearly black, as if her pupils were permanently roused in dilation.

Ever since those meetings in the library, when they mapped out the great Khan's life, Jo longed to tell Laura how he felt about her. When he reached her locker, however, he hesitated. *Should I or shouldn't I* went around in his thoughts like *she loves me, she loves me not*. He took stock in the honour of his intent, adoring Laura the way Romeo did Juliet, a devotion he'd learned from his parents, whom still looked into each other's eyes like love-struck teens. Their deeply affectionate bond was what led them to spell Jo's name without the *e*.

When Igor and Ana Martini emigrated from Slovenia twenty-three winters ago, they spent most of their free time in Canada, cuddled by a woodstove, sipping tea and laughing at each other's mispronunciations till their new language made perfect sense. It was during that period, when their heads were often buried in a dictionary, they came across the word *jo*, of Scottish etymology meaning sweetheart.

Jo took a deep breath and slipped a mauve envelope behind Laura's locker door. After weeks of wrestling with words, he managed to articulate his adoration in a poem:

Dear Laura,

As seen in my dream, I confess
You thrived as a beautiful Princess
Upon a stately steed,
Between supreme oaks
You paid no heed
Cloaked by twilight
Galloping at top speed
Toward a moonless night
Your hair flowed upon the wake
Of growing shadows along a lake
In a mystical mood, I awoke
And did conclude, the myriad way
Of your vast pulchritude
Might never be sufficiently praised
Though the universe of my heart
Would strive, utterly enchanted
If by chance a chance is granted

If my aim seems true, please meet me at four, behind the school.
Sincerely Yours,
Jo Martini

After the letter landed with a thud behind the steel door, Jo scooted away.

The lunch bell sounded and students poured into the hallway. Laura opened her locker and found the letter. As she read the poem, a broad smile lifted her cheeks. But then she saw Jo's name at the bottom and her expression turned sour. She crumpled the paper into a ball and tossed it onto a nearby garbage can.

The instant Laura was out of sight, Dave Needler emerged to pick the letter out of the trash. He leaned against Laura's locker and read: *Beautiful Princess? Stately steed? SUPREME OAKS!* He kicked the locker door with his cowboy boot, ripped the letter into tiny pieces and jammed it back into the garbage.

With "four o'clock behind the school" etched upon his rage, he tromped off to have lunch with his football buddies. Every one of those guys knew one thing for certain: Nobody messed with Dave's sister!

***

Fidgety and wrought with anticipation, Jo waited for Laura behind the school. A long-stemmed rose was pinned inside his jacket, a gift to be bestowed directly from his heart. If only she'd show. His mind flipped continuously between the ecstasy of assignation and the dread of rejection. *Stay positive*, he told himself. *And anyway, if she doesn't show, the sun will still rise tomorrow.*

No matter what he told himself, his heart pounded heavily against his polo shirt pocket. He tried to walk off his angst by pacing ten meters to and fro. At 4:10, he stood crestfallen, gripped by the woeful pangs of unrequited love; but then a shadow emerged from right behind him. He assumed it was Laura, turned to greet her but was shocked and startled. "Oh, hi Dave," he said, trying to regain his composure.

Dave stood in his extra large football jacket, eclipsing the sun. He bared a sliver of teeth through a tight grin. "Laura wants you to meet her at Salem's Bridge."

Barely able to contain his excitement, Jo said, "Okay, thanks."

Dave turned and walked away. *Succinct fellow*, Jo thought. He looked forward to getting to know him. Perhaps they'd double date some time. Jo thought Laura had shown excellent discretion by arranging an alternative venue. Meeting away from the school would allow them to talk more freely, without the scrutiny of peers. A half kilometre path through the forest led to Salem's Bridge.

Entering the woods, Jo pondered the thrilling prospect of meeting Laura at such a private, romantic setting. Although he imagined they'd become intimate on a gradual basis, he couldn't help thinking ahead to subsequent encounters, when he might run his fingers through her immaculate hair, hold her close and kiss her for the first time.

Whoa, slow down, he told himself, I mustn't assume anything! Laura must have exceptional standards—she's probably the most sought after young woman in the school, no the city, no the country! I must prove myself worthy before I…*before I drink from her cup*! He laughed at himself, keenly aware of love's manifest delirium.

He pondered their compatibility. Wonder what she reads? Probably Jane Austen. I bet she prefers live theatre to movies. Wonder what her favourite colour is? On he strolled, eager to fulfill his destiny with the beautiful princess of his dreams.

About a quarter kilometre from civilization, he heard short bursts of running all around him. He stopped and looked circumspectly: a breeze rustled brown leaves between the trees—someone charged out of the brush and rammed a shoulder into his back! Jo fell to the ground and scraped his chin upon a rock. Someone else booted his guts and he struggled to catch his breath.

"Pick him up!" a third guy said. After the first two ruffians lifted Jo to his feet and held him upright, Dave Needler squeezed a pair of leather gloves onto his fists and pummelled Jo as if he were a punching bag. When Needler stopped whaling, Jo spat blood and said, "*WHY ARE YOU DOING THIS*?"

"Stop bothering my sister, or next time I'll have to get rough!"

His pals broke into laughter. Jo was obviously in no position to dispute Dave, but his feelings for Laura overwhelmed his reason. "Don't you think it's up to Laura herself to decide whether she sees me or not?"

Needler tugged on the lip of his leather glove. "Guess I haven't gotten through to you yet." He doubled Jo over with a vicious blow to the solar plexus, then told his pals to strip him naked. They pushed him to the ground and pulled off his clothes. When Dave found the rose inside Jo's coat, he tore the petals off and fixed the thorny stem around the top of Jo's head. "Look fellas—*Jesus*!"

As they broke into fits of laughter, Jo curled into a ball and grew despondent. "One more thing, Martini," Dave said, "If you squeal on us, if you breathe a word of this to anyone, your parents will be killed! Could be a house fire or a beating with baseball bats—so you better keep your mouth shut!"

As if punctuating the threat with exclamation marks, all three boys stomped on his naked body. They were busting him up inside, kicking his head in. Eventually, one of them said, "He's out cold—we better stop before we kill him!" The three football buddies fled through the forest like a pack of wolves.

A couple hours later, Jo regained consciousness but remained perfectly still, as if set in rigor mortis. He lay on his back with his head turned to one side. Through his good eye, the one not swollen shut, he stared into the shadowy forest. Ethereal in the moonlight, Laura emerged in a long white gown. Her eyes were darker than the night, her hair was so sheen, the silky strands glowed with a blue tint.

Stiff as Frankenstein's monster, Jo sat up and extended his arms towards her. Despite everything he had been through, he still longed to hold Laura Needler. Preoccupied with a clump of mud at the bottom of her dress, she cursed the forest and all its filth, then vanished into the crisp, night air. *Be careful what you wish for, you just might get it*? Not even in hallucination was he able to hold her. His arms were locked outright, desperate for her to return, but his madness failed to re-conjure her image.

Meanwhile, Jo's parents were worried sick. When he didn't come home by dinner, they called the police, who wouldn't do anything until Jo was missing for 24 hours. At 8 o'clock, Igor formed a search party comprising neighbours, as well as Anton and Miles. Since nobody had seen Jo around the neighbourhood, they headed into the forest beside his school. Half way into the woods, someone cried out, "Over here!"

Igor, Anton and Miles dashed along the path and found Jo sitting upright at the center of cross-firing flashlights. His naked, battered body maintained a rigid posture. Although his eyes were open and he was blinking, Jo failed to acknowledge their presence.

Igor whipped off his coat and blanketed his son. He untangled the rose stem from his hair. "*What in God's name happened here*? Who did this to you, son?" None of the words penetrated Jo's vacant gaze.

Miles turned white. "It's alright Son," Anton said, "We're all shaken up. Uncle Igor has all the help he needs. Why don't you and I go on ahead and call for help?"

Igor looked up and saw the terror in his nephew's eyes. "Your dad's right. Go ahead and call an ambulance. We'll meet you at the hospital."

When Miles looked into his uncle's eyes, he picked up on an inner strength that superseded the horror. His dad had the same expression, one that said they'd rise above this ordeal no matter what. "I'd like to stay with Jo, if that's alright," Miles said.

Igor directed one of his neighbours to run ahead for help. The rest of the search party fashioned a makeshift stretcher out of four coats. Eight men, four on each side, then picked up the ends of the empty sleeves and hauled Jo down the path. Though the search party maintained a positive front, they couldn't shake the eerie feeling they were trapped in a zombie's nightmare, spooked by Jo's freaky ridged glare.

Meanwhile, Dave Needler was home drinking foreign beer with his buddies. He raised a frosty mug: "Here's to all perverts getting what they deserve!"

One of his buddies, Norm Pattison, was having second thoughts. He'd been Jo's classmate a few times over the years and didn't think he was such a bad guy. Norm thought about an ex-teammate who suffered a broken leg at football practice, the same week he'd asked Laura to a movie. Norm himself was smitten by the raven haired beauty.

Affected by Dutch courage, he thought, I'm Dave's best friend—surely he wouldn't mind if *I* asked her out. But then he noticed the leather gloves on the table, the ones Dave had used to pummel Jo to a pulp. *Just drink the free beer,* he told himself, *and keep your mouth shut*!

Chapter Three

At the same time Jo entered the forest to meet his horrible fate, Miles awaited Sheila Babcock in the front foyer of Perth Bay High. Butterflies were flocking his stomach when she burst through a hallway door, and greeted him with a kiss that lingered on his lips…much longer than when she had kissed him in the morning—it took his breath away!

"Don't worry Miles, I won't bite; *not unless you want me to*."

"Uh, that's okay—if you want to bite something, I'll buy you a burger." He loved the way she squinted when she laughed, as if her eyelids squeezed mirth for all it was worth. While they strolled down Rural Route #66, Sheila reached for his hand. Her touch made his chest feel warm and heavy. Simply being seen with her filled him with delirious pride.

"Where'd you get those big blue eyes?" she asked.

"My dad I guess."

She lifted his hand and examined his lanky fingers like they were precious gem stones. "You have really nice hands."

"Thanks." He wanted to repay a compliment but didn't know where to start.

She asked a series of questions, like where did he learn to play basketball? And, why did he wait so long to try out for the school team? (It occurred to him she must have had a thing for basketball players.) Out of the blue she said, "You sure have a nice body."

"Oh?"

"Well, you're tall and slim and fit and you have a nice butt!"

Her compliment surprised him. Until that moment, he had only ever heard his mother say he was *way* too skinny. By the time they reached Sheila's driveway, he felt more than just comfortable—he felt ten feet tall! "THE BABCOCKS" was written in red paint upon a black mailbox. "It's a long driveway," she said, "We still have a ways to go."

"That's okay, I like walking with you."

While strolling, he noticed the trees and wild shrubbery threatened to overtake the dirt road. He half expected to see a trail of breadcrumbs. "We let the forest grow wild around here" she said, "We like it that way—it's natural."

"Natural is good," he said.

Finally they reached her house, a small bungalow made of limestone. Once inside, Sheila pegged their coats upon hallway hooks. They sat on a sofa together. He took a cursory look and saw a barrage of candles, vases and knickknacks depicting the Dark Ages. Green vines surrounded the room, meticulously hand painted on the top of yellow walls. He thought it was odd there was no TV.

Sheila slung her legs over his lap. He smelled remnants of their walk upon her skin, fresh air mixed with her body heat. Their lips drew near and he braced himself for what promised to be one smouldering kiss—but then the phone rang and a woman (her mother?) called up from the basement, "Sheila, it's for you!"

"I'll be right back," she said. He heard her descend nearby stairs.

Ten minutes later, Miles wondered if Sheila would ever return. Couldn't she speak to whoever-it-was later? To gain patience, he surveyed the knickknacks. There were mud huts with straw roofs;

little men with spears, swords, and maces; and, of course, there were various caldrons tended by women of various ages.

A bead of sweat rolled out his armpit and down his ribs: the room felt hot as a sauna. He pulled off his sweater and felt somewhat refreshed in his T-shirt. Sleep deprived, he got the nods and fought to stay awake; but then the scent of a musky perfume sliced through his ennui and made his hormones hum!

He expected to see Sheila; instead, two Siamese cats pranced into the room, followed by a young woman he'd never seen before. "Hi, I'm Tammy, Sheila's sister."

While he stood and introduced himself, he noticed stark contrasts between the Babcock sisters. Sheila had wavy blond hair; Tammy's was straight and brunette. Sheila had a curvaceous figure; Tammy was tall and willowy. And he'd never seen Sheila wear anything like Tammy's black, knee-high, hooded dress, which she wore with blue stockings and granny boots. On the other hand, both girls had beautiful brown eyes. He also recognized the same kicky, carefree smile in Tammy that was blatant in Sheila. Perhaps they were half sisters.

Tammy sat on a loveseat kitty-corner to the sofa, so that their knees were nearly touching. Meanwhile, the cats were rubbing themselves wildly against his shins and calves. He nodded at them. "Those are mighty, frisky pussies uh, cats you have there."

She laughed. "Yeah, but it was my sister who dragged you in here!"

He laughed. "As in, *look what the cat dragged in*—very funny!"

"You're probably wondering why you haven't seen me at school. I've been home schooled by my mother."

"Didn't know there was such a thing." He remembered the rumours about Sheila having a sister in an asylum, tried to size up her sanity.

Before the silence grew too thick, she said, "Are you dating Sheila?"

"Well, not yet…we just met."

Her flirtatious smile and eyebrow cock made him blush. Did she think he was up for grabs?

"Where are my manners?" she said, "Would you like something to drink?"

He accepted in earnest. His throat was parched. She left the room briefly and returned with two gothic goblets, filled with orangey-yellow liquid. "Cheers," she said. They clinked goblets together.

He quenched his thirst with a big gulp. "This stuff's *delicious*, what is it?"

"Peach and peyote juice."

Of course he was familiar with peaches. But peyote? As if reading his mind she said, "Peyote juice comes from a cactus."

He chugged every drop. Moments later, they were smiling at each other for no apparent reason. No longer did they need to speak to feel comfortable; both teens seemed elated simply to exist. It was getting dark outside. Tammy lit several candles, the scent of nutmeg and cinnamon, reminding him of pumpkin pie. Then she started to sway.

That's odd, he thought, she's dancing without music, as if her hips were in sync with silent rhythms of the universe—whoa!—*Silent rhythms of the universe*? What to hell am I talking about? Who said that?

He might have freaked out except Tammy was so calm and at ease with herself, as if lucid dream states were natural. Preferable even.

Candlelight flickered about the room like a clan of dancing devils. The vines painted on the walls fluttered like streamers in wind.

Before he could entangle himself in a thick web of introspection, Tammy gestured for him to join her. He refused, waving her off. With the bottom of her dress slipping and sliding across her blue stockings, she stepped around the coffee table and stood directly before him. Next thing he knew, he was on his feet, gyrating around the living room.

He was at best a shaky dancer. Without music, he was completely lost. Not that Tammy noticed, consumed as she was by her own melodic movements. She brushed up against him and locked her fingers behind his neck. He set his hands upon her hips.

What if Sheila sees us like this? he wondered. *We're only dancing*. Waltzing made it easier for him to find rhythm. Then again, when it came to slow dancing, his technique was limited to one, continuous pivot that spun them around in circles. Before long, he couldn't distinguish if it was him or the room that was spinning.

He broke away from her and collapsed upon the sofa. The vines on the walls now zoomed around the room, as if caught in a jet stream. "The wind in here is weird," he said, "But I get it: *the wind is your friend*."

She chuckled. "What do you mean Miles?"

"It was the flow of your dress—the bottom of your dress—that drew a gust all around us—sort of scary but extraordinary!"

"Are you into poetry Miles?"

"Not really." After a few seconds, he added, "But I have a cousin who is."

She plopped down beside him, placed her hand upon his chest and felt his racing heart. "Don't worry. You're not going crazy or anything, just trippin' a little. Lie back and try to relax. I'll—" Her voice echoed in his thoughts as he passed out.

***

Miles awoke in pitch darkness, thinking he'd fallen asleep at home. When he sat up on the sofa, someone straddled his lap! He felt the bottom of a dress land upon his hands. Whoever-it-was leaned forward and soft strands of hair rained upon his face, causing shivers to erect across his cheeks, to his ears and down his spine.

Instinctively, he slid his hands under her skirt and upon her hips. She tossed her head from side to side, whipping him gently with her long, soft hair, and his shivers burst into full-blown goose bumps. Then he remembered—Sheila! Or was it Tammy? The hair is long and straight: *It's Tammy— NOT COOL*! In one reflexive motion, he pushed her aside and jumped up—***BANG!*** He smashed his shin against the coffee table and fell back upon the sofa. Pain shot through his leg and snapped him out of his trance. The flickering candlelight reignited to reveal Tammy laying horizontally, levitated above the coffee table. A choir in the dark chanted, "*ROE, NUUE, ISHH, BACHH, DARR*…"

Robotically, Tammy turned her head to face him—her eyes rolled back in her head! Horrified, he thought, *I'm still dreaming*! He squeezed his eyelids together, and when he opened them again, the lights were on and both sisters were sitting on the loveseat, reading rustic magazines.

Sheila glanced at him. "*Have a nice nap*?"

He sat up. "Yeah, hope you didn't mind. I was up early and—"

"It's alright, Miles," Tammy said, "We all get a little crazy sometimes." Her gaze fell back upon the magazine.

Miles felt like he was overstaying his welcome. His inclination to leave grew urgent when a wave of nausea wracked his guts. He fought the impulse to make a mad dash for the door. "Well, I should be going." As he pulled on his sweater, a bead of sweat trickled down his forehead and sopped his brow.

After Miles and Tammy said goodbye to each other, Sheila walked him to the front door. "Thanks for having me," he said.

She pulled him close and whispered, "Hope you had a good time—but don't tell anyone about my sister. Okay?"

"Is she in some sort of trouble?" he said while slipping into his coat.

"As you already know, she can be heaven or she can be hell. Mother thinks it's best to limit her exposure to the outside world." She kissed him on the cheek and said, "See ya on Friday."

He wanted to know, why Friday? but burst outside, ducked behind an evergreen and heaved his guts out! Cold November air refreshed his lungs and cleared his head. He had lost track of time—his mother was probably having fits! By moonlight, he jogged back to school, retrieved his bike, then stood on the pedals for maximum torque.

As he sped through the intermittent glow of streetlights, he wondered how much of the evening was real, versus how much he had dreamt. His shin was definitely throbbing. Was it from banging into the coffee table, or did he have shin splints from all the running he'd done that day? He'd check for bruising when he got home. The peyote juice certainly bolstered his stereotype of witches as being spooky.

Before long, he dropped his bike in front of his house and stepped inside. Betty ran over and hugged him. "Thank God you're all right!" She pushed him back and slapped the side of his head. "Where have you been? We've been worried sick!"

"I was at a basketball practice."

His father said, "You made the team then? Way to go! How'd the shoes fit?"

"They were awesome dad—thanks! And yes, I made the team!"

"That's great, son. You need to call your mother, though, if you're going to be late."

"Okay, for sure. Dad, what are you doing home from work?"

"Jo is missing. We'd assumed the two of you were together. Grab something quick to eat. We're going to help your Uncle with his search party."

***

Miles crawled into bed at daybreak. Although he'd been awake for twenty-four hours (other than his "nap" at Sheila's house), he couldn't sleep, haunted by horrific visions of Jo's eerie gaze. Betty popped her head into his room, "Can't sleep?"

"You should have seen Jo, mom. He looked like the living dead."

Betty gave Miles one of her mild tranquilizers. Seconds after taking the pill, he fell into such a deep sleep, not even the Babcock sisters could have roused him.

Chapter Four

Two evenings after Jo Martini was pulverized and left naked in the forest, the Needler's were having dinner at their mansion. The family of four sat at the end of a mahogany table, big enough to seat twenty.

A weary, middle-aged woman served a bottle of red wine that was older than herself. When she reached around David Sr., she stubbed her toe on his chair and spilt a drop of the wine into his soup. Mr. Needler slammed his Scotch glass on the table. "Get control of your hoofs or I'll send you back to Guadalajara, or wherever the hell it was you came from!"

"Yes sir, sorry sir." She scurried back to the kitchen and burst into tears.

Dave didn't look up from his sports magazine, but chuckled under his breath. With his new brush-cut and steely blue eyes, he was the spitting image of his father.

Harrietta, Laura's svelte, olive skinned mother, dabbed the corner of her lip with a serviette, then said, "Do you think you could ease up on the help? They're not easy to replace, you know. It took me five weeks to find Martha. She came highly recommended."

David Sr. grumbled something incomprehensible.

Laura ignored her stepfather's rage. He never directed it towards his adopted princess. She simply tuned him out whenever he lost his temper.

Harrietta noticed her husband was now sitting obliquely to the table, staring off into space. "What's eating you this evening?" she said.

"Nothing." However, a telltale vein throbbed across his temple. Perhaps his foul mood stemmed from the union leaders at his plant, whose "bleeding hearts" constantly stuck in his craw. Or maybe he was peeved again about his wife's career as a legal secretary. Since they obviously didn't need the money, he thought she was foolish and defiant working fifty hours a week with a fleet of flirty lawyers.

He had met Harrietta in 1969, at the very law firm he now despised. Berger & Kerr, Corporate Law defended his textile company against a breach of safety regulations. The plaintiff, a forty-seven year old father of three, had lost a finger while operating a machine overdue for maintenance. Dave Sr. joked with Harrietta that the employee had *given Needler Inc. the finger*! After a brief affair, they ditched their respective spouses and married each other, a union so upwardly mobile for Harrietta, it made her feel like Jackie Onassis.

"Who'd ya bet on, Dallas or Miami?" Dave Jr. asked his dad, snapping him out of his dark meditation.

Football talk was Harrietta's cue to branch off with her daughter. "Your father and I went to the Webster's for dinner last night and Dorothy showed me a blouse she bought in Montreal for $75. I thought, where will she wear it? Around the house vacuuming? I could wear something like that to work; but for her, it's a complete waste of money!"

Laura laughed and said, "Her daughter certainly can't be accused of overdressing. I swear she does most of her shopping at Bargain Barney's!"

The servant returned with the main course. Both father and son had had their steaks cooked rare, bleeding on their plates!

Laura's portions were slight: four green beans, half a baked potato and a sliver of beef. After eating, she excused herself and headed upstairs. In her room, she sprayed French perfume around her canopy bed. After a deep breath, she thought, God I love that fragrance—nothing subtle about it! She pulled a fashion magazine off her night table and carefully scrutinized its glossy photos.

Several minutes later, there was a knock at her door. Before she could answer, Dave Jr. barged in and sat beside her on the bed. She pointed to the picture of a slinky, blue dress. "Do you think I'd look good in that?"

"Very sexy," he said. "You know, you're prettier than any of those models and I'm not saying it just to be nice."

"Since when have you ever been nice?"

He laughed. "Want to see my all time favourite bathing suit?"

"It's not exactly swimwear season but okay, show me."

He darted to his room and returned with an old issue of *Vogue* magazine. He flipped through and stopped at a bright red, Ralph Lauren bikini. "Remember this?"

"Of course. I wore it last year when we went to Mexico."

"Remember that idiot who walked into the pier because he couldn't take his eyes off you?"

They shared a laugh together. Then silence.

"I have a confession to make," he said. "I've been kinda obsessed with you ever since that thing happened to us in Cancun."

Reflecting upon their terrifying ordeal made their hearts flutter with racy beats. Dave slid his hand under her skirt and calluses he'd earned in the weight room tugged on her nylons. She gasped. Her life was like a house of cold, empty rooms; but now, sparks flew along a private corridor, promising to fill a lonely void with intense heat. She told him to go lock her door and it was one of the few times Dave Needler took orders from anyone.

Chapter Five

On the Friday following his beating, Jo Martini remained motionless in a hospital bed. A young nurse checked his intravenous, then propped him up against his pillows. "You have company, dear. That nice young man is here again." She didn't expect a response. Jo remained obviously oblivious.

The nurse smiled at Miles as she passed him on her way out of the room. He sat on a chair next to the bed and waited for Jo to blink, one of the few signs of life he'd relinquish. "Hi, Jo. Still on the mend, eh? The doctor says you're in a catatonic stupor. Whatever that means. It has something to do with 'bizarre, ridged behaviour.' I don't know much about it. What I do know is that I miss my best friend."

Jo stared at the washroom, directly across the foot of his bed. The bruises on his face had faded from dark blue to pale green.

"There's something I've been dying to tell you: I went to Sheila's house on Tuesday. You were right about her—she's into witchcraft! And her sister, Tammy, wow—what a trip, talk about *a walk on the wild side*! She had me under some kind of spell; or, maybe it was this strange juice she gave me." He explained his difficulty in distinguishing his dreams from what really happened.

"Ever since the weird visit to her house, Sheila's been hot and cold towards me. I didn't see her on Wednesday because she skipped school. Yesterday, she ignored me and I thought, Oh well, guess it's already over between us. But then this morning, she kissed me at my locker and invited me to a party at her house, so I'll be seeing her tonight. I wonder if I'm suppose to go as Sheila's date or just a friend. And what about her sister? Guess I'll avoid her at all costs.

“You have to snap out of this trance, Jo. I need your advice on another matter. Sure, I made the basketball team, but the coach benched me during our first exhibition game. What’s the point of running my ass off in practices if I don’t get to play in the games? And I’m tired of the pranks my team-mates play on me. I was already nervous before the game when I noticed my new running shoes were missing. I looked all over, finally found them out in the gym—at centre court! When I came back into the change room, everyone was laughing at me!

“I don’t know, Jo. Maybe I should just quit. What do you think? I could sure use your advice.” Miles looked at the plastic tube plugged into his cousin’s vein. “I suppose my problems are minor compared to yours.”

After sitting with Jo for an hour, Miles said, “I have to get ready for the party. But I’ll be back tomorrow.” He gave his cousin a brief hug, then cycled home.

Later in the shower, he shampooed his hair twice, then applied conditioner. Thinking he might be naked with a woman for the first time in his life, he wanted to be perfectly clean, scrubbed every inch of his body till his skin turned lobster red.

His mother banged on the door. “YOU’RE RUNNING UP THE WATER BILL! GET OUT OF THERE—NOW!”

“I CAN’T HEAR YOU, I’M IN THE SHOWER.”

Betty stormed down the hallway and said to Anton, “Not long ago you couldn’t get him into the shower—now you can’t get him out!”

Miles knew his mother wanted him out of the shower but he wasn’t done perfecting his hygiene. He massaged banana shampoo onto his pubic hair, rinsed, and was about to apply conditioner when Betty pounded on the door again. "IF YOU DON'T SHUT THE WATER OFF THIS INSTANT, YOU'LL BE GROUNDED!"

In his haste to crank the faucets off, Miles nearly pulled his groin as he slipped on the soapy tub floor. After brushing his hair, he dashed to his room and pulled on the tartan shirt his aunt Daunusa had given him last year for Christmas. As usual, he rolled back the cuffs so nobody would notice the sleeves were five inches too short. He stepped into his favourite TEK jeans, the ones sent to him by his Slovenian grandmother.

Socks were a problem. He'd used all his white ones playing basketball and had to choose between a pair of colourful argyles and black dress socks. He went with the argyles. He galloped to the front closet and slipped into his jean jacket. On his way out the door, Betty reminded him of his curfew.

Miles cycled to rural route #66. When he neared Sheila's driveway a series of motorcycles and souped-up cars passed him like a convoy. He stopped at the Babcock's mailbox and realized his armpits were soaked with sweat! *So much for all that meticulous showering*! No need to panic, he thought, I can fix this. He opened his jacket, unbuttoned his shirt and faced the wind. As a chilly twilight breeze cooled him down and dried his perspiration, people who passed on the highway gave him funny looks. In a matter of moments, he was all aired out, his hygiene completely restored. He buttoned up his shirt, then cruised down the long, unkempt driveway.

Motorcycles were strewn about the front yard. A dozen or so late-model cars were parked along the laneway. Miles leaned his bike against a tree, then passed a crowd to reach the front porch. When he knocked on the door, a heavyset bearded fellow sitting on the stoop said, “Hey man, you don’t have to knock, just walk in.”

Sheila opened the door anyway. Most everything about her was black: her mascara, her nail polish, her dress, her shoes. She kissed him on the cheek and hung up his coat. “There’s beer in the fridge,” she said, then disappeared into a throng.

He didn’t want to follow her like a puppy, so he went to the kitchen and pulled a bottle of Brador beer out of the fridge. He felt out of place standing in a house full of people, talking to none of them. He heard music coming from the basement, “Bohemian Rhapsody” by Queen, the rock song infused with measures of opera. Miles followed Freddie Mercury’s wailing vocals down the stairs.

The descent was dimly lit by the distant glow of candlelight. He tapped his toe past the last step to assure himself he had reached the bottom. At the end of a hallway, he could see the candlelight emanated from behind beaded streamers. Must be the rec room, he thought.

He passed the silhouettes of three doors and two couples making out. When he reached the end of the hall, he parted the streamers and they seemed to come alive—*like startled snakes*—clutching his wrist and forearm! As he flailed and gyrated, his entanglement worsened: the beads had now latched onto both his arms! “Watch it man—you’re spilling beer on us!” someone said from the other side.

Flustered, Miles ripped the streamers off the threshold and beads flew every which way. Everyone stopped what they were doing and stared at him in the candlelight. A long haired fellow pointed to the floor and said, “*Beans, man*, *magic beans*!”

They all burst into laughter. Miles didn’t know which way to look. He was about to bolt back up the stairs when a warm, familiar voice said, "Don't worry Miles, people are always getting tangled up in those things. Come and sit with us."

The crowd parted like the Red Sea, revealing Tammy, who sat in a circle with four scruffy fellows in leather vests. They surrounded a huge glass pipe set upon a shag carpet. When Miles sat beside Tammy, she kissed him on his cheek. *So much for avoiding her at all costs*, he thought. It unnerved him that the guys sitting with her were several years his senior.

Like her sister, Tammy was dressed in a black dress. Her eyes were glassy and puffy. She passed him one of the rubber mouthpieces. "Smoke this," she said, "It'll help you relax."

When Miles hauled on the mouthpiece, the glass pipe bubbled like boiling water. Before long, a placid wave of euphoria softened his fierce self-consciousness. He noticed the guys in the circle had parked their riding boots beside themselves. He did the same with his running shoes, then crossed his legs and sipped what was left of his beer.

A guy sitting across from Miles said, "What was I jabbering about…oh yeah, school's a total scam, *man*. The government uses it to programme little kids. And teacher's don't give a damn, *man*. They're only in it for their paycheques."

Miles thought the guy sort of made sense. But then Tammy flashed a smile at him, so Miles felt compelled to argue. "I don't think school's a scam…man—it's good to crack a book every now and then. One of my favourites is *Don Quixote*. It's about this knight—"

"*This night*?" another guy said, "*A book about tonight*? *Far out, man!*"

"NO! A knight, you know, a guy with a sword, on a horse, wearing armour. The book is about Don Quixote, a knight who is in love with a princess who is beautiful and perfect in every way, except she's a figment of his imagination."

The group of stoners seemed lost in thought. Miles hauled on the pipe, quite pleased with himself, feeling like a little professor. But then the guy he disputed said, "Hey man, you don't have to go to school to read a book. You can go to the library."

"Yeah, but, teachers help us understand what we're reading."

"Teachers oppress more than they help, man. *Kids can't even go pee without permission*! It's all part of a grand scam, man, and..."

Tammy laced up her granny boots and headed down the hallway. WAIT! Miles thought, WHERE ARE YOU GOING? She'd been his security blanket. The volume of yammering voices surrounding him grew into a cacophony of sound bites. He swallowed the last few drops of his beer, then didn't know what to do with his hands. He took it out on the pipe. After several puffs, he tucked his thighs against his chest and hugged his knees, a sort of upright fetal position.

A rotund bearded fellow sitting next to Miles said, "*Nice socks, man*!"

"Thanks," Miles managed to say. But then he realised, *It wasn't a compliment—he's making fun of my argyles!*

The guy Miles had argued with said, "All those blue and red diamonds, man…(he tilted his head from side to side)…your socks are like… *kaleidoscopes*!"

As they burst into laughter, Miles wanted to crawl under the carpet and die! Again he took it out on the pipe. But then the mouthpiece went mushy between his lips. He looked down the stem, which was now the slimy limb of a cycloptic octopus—staring up at him, baring a single fang! Seized by a massive panic attack, Miles spat the fleshy arm out of his mouth. He wanted to run out of the house, but his body felt heavy as stoned. He grabbed his shoes, forced himself to his feet and staggered out of the room.

When he entered the hallway, it spun like a funhouse tunnel. Dizzy and faint, the stairs seemed insurmountable. He dragged his shoulder along the wall, then ducked into a room. In pitch darkness, he bumped his hip against a piece of furniture, found a bed and collapsed.

He wasn't sure how much time had elapsed when a lamp beside the bed shined in his eyes. He squinted at Sheila, who tossed her dress aside, her voluptuous breasts bulging from a lacy black bra. Somehow, he was under the blankets—naked!

She slipped under the blankets, kissed him madly, then leaned on her elbow and sang in a deep, operatic voice: "*OH MAMA MIA, MAMA MIA LET ME GO! BLEEZEBUB HAS A DEVIL PUT ASIDE FOR ME!"*

"'Bohemian Rhapsody,' right? That song was playing when I came downstairs."

She sang, "*Nothing really matters, anyone can see. Nothing really matters. Nothing really matters to me-e-e-e*."

She stopped singing and said, "If the Universe were a glass castle, life would mean less than a grain of sand."

"Glass and sand…life's fragile like glass, and fleeting like sand in an hour-glass. Is that what you mean, Sheila?"

She reached into a night table, pulled out a razorblade and sliced her left forearm, from wrist to biceps. An old boot popped out of her arm, followed by a fish head. Miles watched in horror, till his pounding heart awoke him with a jolt! He caught his breath and thanked God it was just a dream. Wait a minute, he thought, where are my clothes? It was still pitch dark. Who's this on my arm, Sheila or Tammy? He didn't care any more! He leaned over and planted his lips on whoever-it-was and she kissed him right back. He explored with his finger tips: long, straight hair…small, pert breasts…Tammy—it was Tammy!

So be it, he thought. He kissed down her neck and slid the blankets down to her hips. She caressed his hair and moaned with pleasure while he licked and sucked her nipples, hard as bullets. He kissed his way back to her mouth and when their tongues met, it was all over for him, the warmth of his Milky Way pooled across her abdomen. He fell back to his side of the bed. "Sorry," he said, "It's my first time."

"Don't worry Miles. It was nice."

She used the corner of the sheet to clean up, then lit a cigarette. The door creaked open and a ceiling light flicked on. Sheila peeked into the room—the light went out and the door slammed shut! Fed up with Sheila's hot and cold whimsy, he said, "So what's going on here? Do sister witches always switch guys like this?"

"You and I hit it off. My sister happened to bring us together. So?"

He didn't know what to say.

"Your wheels are turning, aren't they?"

"I just thought Sheila…never mind. Will I ever see you again?"

She sighed and sat on the edge of the bed.

"Alright," he said, "No more questions. Whatever happens, happens."

She opened the drawer of a night table and pulled out a condom. "Here," she said, "This will help you last longer."

By the witching hour, Miles had filled the reservoir tip of three condoms. He would have loved to spend the entire night with her, but didn't want to face his mother in the morning. "It must be getting late," he said, "I'd better be going." As they dressed, he said, "Guess this is it then; I'll never see you again?"

Refusing to respond, she pulled her boot on.

"Alright. That's cool," he said, trying to be cool. "I just want you to know that I think you're beautiful. I hope you don't mind me saying so."

"Why would I mind, Miles? Thanks."

He couldn't get over her nonchalance. Once dressed, he kissed her goodbye and climbed the stairs. The house was still full of revellers. Sheila was nowhere to be found. He buttoned up his jean jacket, stepped outside, then pedaled in a blissful state of afterglow. At long last, all that fretting about his virginity had come to an end—it wasn't a life sentence after all! A heady sense of relief heightened his elation.

He wondered how it would be when he saw Sheila again at school. "Hope you don't mind," he imagined saying, "But I screwed your sister!" He laughed so hard, he nearly fell off his bike. But then the cold bit into his mirth and made his eyes water and it sank in that Sheila would never be his girlfriend. Even though her affection had been erratic, he was going to miss her casual kisses, the highlight of his school week, ever since that magical morning when she first planted her pouty lips upon him. Too late to worry about that now, he thought—*damn it! What have I done?*

Chapter Six

Miles visited his cousin Saturday night, the extent of his social life, a stark contrast to the party he had attended at Sheila's house a mere 24 hours ago. He struggled to prop Jo up against his pillows. The spacey eyed patient now had shoulder length hair and a beard beyond the scruffy look. With Jo lugged into an upright position, Miles sat in a chair beside the bed.

After a brief summary of Sheila's party, Miles said, "I know how you like the artsy fartsy stuff, Jo, so I tried to write it all down in a poem." He took out a piece of paper and read:

Upon a wicked crush
My yearning heart did gush
For a Wicca bombshell
Named Sheila Babcock
Who cast a spell
With the mirth of her big brown eyes
And the girth of her flirty smile
She made me blush
With a rush of fool's blood
Tooled for the tunnel of love

But then her sister took me over
A whole other type of conjurer
We smoked the spook pipe together
Till my mouth and knees turned to mush
With a curse of the octopus
Whose evil eye conspired to ply us

I could have done worse
Than to lie with Tammy
A grand one night stand
But now I'm sorry
For I adored Sheila more than I knew
And will miss her through and through

Woe is my odyssey
Woe is my Oddity,
To have arms too long for my body
Longing to hold the waning Witch
Who pawned me off without a glitch!

So you see Jo, I have been listening to you all these years. Had my head stuck in a dictionary all day—you would have been proud! Never knew words could be so addictive. Sure makes the time fly. Has this sort of thing ever happened to you? I'd be looking up one word, only to be distracted by others, with cool definitions, like *doff*, which means to remove clothes; and *amatory*, the expression of sexual love."

Just then, a young cleaning lady popped into the room. She glanced at Jo and said, "Poor fellow. He's lucky to have a friend like you."

"Oh, thanks."

Flowing blond hair, candescent blue eyes, normally such a beautiful woman would have made Miles nervous; but something in the warmth of her smile put him at ease. "Don't mind me," she said, "I'm here to clean." She sprayed solvent onto one of the two picture windows in the room, then started to buff.

Miles spoke to Jo in a whisper. "Tammy was amazing. But I'll sure miss Sheila. In fact, she's all I can think about right now. I'm so confused!" He stared into his cousin's vacant eyes and imagined what Jo might say: *Don't worry, Miles—in the long run, you're better off without either one of them!*

"You might be right, Jo. But what if I'm in love with Sheila? I mean, I really like her. If only there were a way I could win her back."

The young cleaning lady touched Miles on the shoulder. "Sorry dear, visiting hours are over."

"Already? Alright, I'll just say good-bye."

She smiled and went back to work.

"The doctor says people with your condition can have a 'spontaneous recovery.' It's what we're all hoping for." Miles hugged his cousin good-bye and it was like embracing rigor mortis his body was so rigid.

As soon as he left the room, the cleaning lady jammed the chair under the doorknob. She then pulled Jo's blankets off, yanked the intravenous out of his arm, stripped him naked and rolled him onto his stomach. Bruises about his body had faded to dim shadows.

The cleaning lady pulled a small plastic bottle out of her blue apron pocket, squeezed a zigzag of lotion all over his back, then spread the oily extract with a cursory rub. Once his flesh had been warmed, she jumped onto the bed and straddled him.

With strong, deep-penetrating fingers, she kneaded the muscles at the bottom of his skull and down his neck. She worked her way into his trapezius and around his shoulder blades. His tissues in these areas were riddled with tight knots. She prodded each lumpy mass, till they were squashed out of existence.

Next, she leaned down and dragged her elbows along both sides of his spine. His muscles, the *erector spinae*, were locked like rows of clamped vice grips. Her first pass down his back most certainly would have made him cry out with ecstasy if he had been fully conscious. Several deep passes dissolved the gridlock along his backbone.

She jumped off the bed and checked for a reaction: all he did was breathe and blink. She rolled him over, covered his genitals with a corner of the sheet, then squeezed lotion onto his chest. There was a bang on the door and a nurse yelled to the front desk, "THE DOOR'S STUCK AGAIN, CALL MAINTENANCE!"

The cleaning lady's brilliant blue eyes intensified. She jumped back onto Jo and sunk her fingertips into his pectoral tissues, stiff as tangled tree roots, especially above his heart. As she prodded feverishly, a maintenance man hammered on the door. A bead of perspiration fell from her brow and splashed upon Jo's lips. Despite her vigorous kneading, his eyes remained fixed. With tears streaming her cheek, she sat back and whispered, "Sorry dear, perhaps in another lifetime."

She slipped the dressing gown back over his body, tucked him under the blankets, then reinserted the intravenous into his arm. The maintenance man must have retrieved a sledgehammer because his blows now shook the room. The cleaning lady stepped backwards, away from the bed. Before she faded into the darkness of the washroom, a sleepy voice said, "*Where are you going? I was just getting into it!*"

She smiled and said, "Welcome back. Enjoy your new gift!"

"Gift? What gift?"

One more thundering bash and the chair flew out from under the doorknob. As a throng of hospital staff flooded into the room, the cleaning lady ducked out the door behind them. The head nurse could see Jo was coherent. She ran over and hugged him. Jo tried to push her aside, but was too weak. "Please get off me," he said, "There's someone hiding in the washroom!"

One of the nurses went into the washroom and flicked the light switch. "Sorry dear, there's nobody here."

"Please—help me up!" He yanked the intravenous out of his arm.

A doctor stared at him in utter amazement. "It's alright, son. You were probably dreaming as you came to."

"Could somebody PLEASE help me to the washroom!"

"Sure," the doctor said, "there's no harm in seeing for yourself."

A couple of nurses helped Jo out of bed. When he looked into the washroom, he couldn't believe his eyes. "I wasn't dreaming—I'm sure of it! A cleaning lady was in my room. She was blond with beautiful blue eyes, about five feet tall."

"Five foot two? Eyes of blue? Scooby, doobie, doobie do?" joked the doctor.

The nurses chuckled. Jo scowled.

"Sorry, Jo," the doctor said, "Your recovery is so overwhelming, it makes me a bit giddy! Seriously though, the woman you saw might have seemed real, but let's not forget how vivid dreams can be."

While the nurses helped Jo back into bed, he said, "I know it sounds crazy, but the cleaning lady is an expert masseuse."

"Expert masseuse, eh?" the head nurse said, "We must find this woman—my neck's been stiff all shift!"

The hospital staff laughed again. "Seriously!" Jo said, "When the cleaning lady massaged me, it was as if she took a chunk of cold steel and molded it into warm clay!"

One of the other nurses said, "You know, Audrey was doing the windows this evening; she fits Jo's description."

"Okay, that explains it," the doctor said, "You see, Jo, people with catatonia can be aware of their surroundings, even when they're in a deep trance. You must have seen Audrey when she was cleaning, then dreamt the part about her massaging you."

"Would it make you feel better," the head nurse said, "if I brought her here, so you could see for yourself?"

"I'd appreciate that."

The cleaning lady was paged and when she entered the room, Jo's face lit up. "It's you! Tell them about the massage you gave me—they think I dreamt it!"

Audrey turned beet red. "There must be some misunderstanding—I cleaned the windows in here and then left."

"Why would you deny what you did for me? It was like a miracle!"

"Sorry dear, you must have been dreaming."

Jo wanted to yell out, STOP LYING! but voices in his head were questioning his sanity. He could have sworn he heard the doctor thinking about which psychiatric drug to administer, meds that mostly ended with *pam*, like diazepam and lorazepam. He also heard Audrey asking him to please stop. "Okay, I must have been dreaming," Jo said, "Sorry to trouble you Ma'am."

She winked at him, then left.

"My throat is dry and I'm hungry," Jo said, "Could I please have ice cream?"

"How 'bout a strawberry sundae?" one of the nurses said.

"That would be perfect!"

The nurse gleefully headed to the kitchen. Another nurse poured Jo a glass of water as the doctor sat on the side of his bed. "It's amazing how vivid dreams can be," he said while pumping a blood pressure cuff. "It reminds me of a query once pondered by the French philosopher, Rene Descartes."

"I know the one you mean, Doc: When you're dreaming, you almost always think you're awake; so when you're awake, how can you be sure you're not dreaming?"

"Yes, very good, you must be well read." The doctor pointed a penlight at Jo's eye and asked him to look to the right. When Jo looked away, he spotted Audrey standing in the doorway. She smiled, then vanished amid the beam of bright light.

Chapter Seven

Friday after school, Laura Needler sat in a booth with three of her friends, at Gourmet Burger. The girls were discussing their plans for higher education, post graduation. Laura and Mercedes planned to stay home and attend Queen's University.

"I think university is overrated," Wendy Weaver said. With her black, coarse hair, she looked like Lucy, the Peanuts character, only she dressed much finer in her Jordache Jeans and angora sweater. "My brother's a psyc. major at U of T and you should hear the nonsense he comes home with. For instance, he says women walk around with a chip on their shoulder because of something called 'penis envy.' He actually believes us girls feel inferior because none of us has a dick!"

"That's disgusting!" Mercedes Mendez said.

"*Penis envy*?" Laura said in disbelief. "I bet whoever dreamt that up was a man. And judging by the way guys gawk, *breast envy* is more like it!"

Laura's third friend, Valerie Doberman, had been sitting in quiet contemplation. But then her red freckled cheeks perked as she smirked and said, "I know of a penis you'd all envy! Guess who has the biggest schlong at our school?"

"How would you know?" Mercedes said, "Have you seen every dick at Perth Bay High?"

"Well, no; but if there's a bigger one out there, I'd like to see it!"

The girls tried to guess who Valerie was talking about. Eventually, Wendy said, "Is it the guy you went out with for a while over the summer—what's his name—he's on the football team…Norm Pattison?"

"Yes, that's him!" Valerie said, "Or as I like to call him, *Enormous Norm.* He's so big, it hurt when we did it, but felt really good. Know what I mean? Probably not."

"Come on, you're exaggerating," Mercedes said. "They're roughly all the same size, aren't they? How big can one get anyway?"

Laura wondered if Dave was big, small or what? Wendy said, "You're kinda quiet Laura. What do you think, does size matter?"

Laura obliterated Dave from her thoughts. "A bigger house is better than a smaller one. A bigger yacht is better, as is a bigger diamond. Clearly, bigger is better!"

As her friends murmured unanimous agreement, Laura found herself squeezing her inner thighs together. Since grade nine, Norm had been sneaking peeks at her when Dave wasn't looking. She never thought much of it; but now, a steamy passion had been stirred, similar to her lust for must-have fashion.

"He's your brother's best friend, isn't he Laura?" Wendy said.

"I was just thinking, he's at our house all the time."

"Well," Wendy said, "Maybe you could set me up with him?"

"Don't count on it. I never get involved with my brother's friends."

"That's smart," Mercedes said, "There might be a fight or a messy break-up, and you could get caught in the middle."

Though Laura agreed, she was already plotting alone time with Norm.

***

The following Saturday, Laura knew Norm would come home with Dave after their workout. They'd stop to have dinner, then come over to play pool and drink beer. While slipping into a sleek new skirt, she contemplated her sexual encounter with Dave, the one that took place *right there* in her canopy bed. Surely, he didn't think it would lead to an ongoing relationship. For starters, his father would murder them both!

She knew for certain she didn't love Dave. Most of the time he repulsed her. *The incident in Mexico created a weird bond between us,* she reasoned, *it got physical—once, one time only, never again! Best to pretend it never happened.*

Laura heard the clunking of shoes falling in the front foyer. She hustled down the back stairs and into the games room. When the two football buddies walked in on Laura, they had a side view of her, bent over the pool table lining up a shot. Below her cherry coloured blouse, she wore a black skirt with a liberal slit on the side. Her long slender legs, in sheer nude stockings, were perched upon black high heeled shoes, with thin straps buckled across her ankles.

Dave furrowed his brows. "A little overdressed for hangin' around the house, aren't you?"

"Can't decide on this outfit. Thought I'd wear it for a while to see if I should keep it or take it back."

"It's a keeper—*For sure!*" Norm said, taking eyefuls of her.

"Who asked you, knucklehead?" Dave said.

"Nobody. Just sayin'. "

"It's settled then," Laura said, "I'll keep it for sure. Thanks Norm."

Dave went to the bar and cracked open a couple of Heinekens.

"Will you be joining us for pool, Laura?" Norm said.

"No, Norm," Dave snapped, "Bye Sis."

"I'll leave you boys to your game," she said on her way out of the room. She knew her brother would get rid of her like that. She let him loosen up with a couple of beers, then returned twenty minutes later with a cocktail in each hand. "I thought you might like something with a little more kick."

"You thought right!" Dave said.

She handed one drink to her brother, the other to Norm. After sipping, Dave said, "Whoa—Sis—this is delicious! Rum punch right?"

"Thought you'd like it."

Norm also thanked her. She turned around to leave. Dave said, "Could you mix us another, in about ten minutes?"

"Sure."

"And maybe you'd like to play a little pool with us."

"*If you want me to*."

When she returned with a refill, Dave was bouncing off the walls. He'd cranked up his favourite album, *Back in Black,* and was playing air guitar. Norm wasn't nearly as animated. He said to Dave, "Do you want to play another game?"

Dave gulped a belt of punch, then said, "You know, this is great! I mean, here I am on Saturday night (belch) with my two favourite people in the world—it just doesn't get better than this!"

Norm raised his brows in disbelief of his friend's uncharacteristic sentimentality. "So, we're done playing pool?"

"You guys go ahead. I'm into the music." Dave jumped around the room, screeching lyrics to "Hells Bells."

Laura racked the balls. "Go ahead Norm, break."

Norm drew back his cue and smashed the balls around the table. When it was Laura's turn, she miscued. "I hate when that happens! What am I doing wrong?"

Norm glanced at his football buddy, who was still playing air guitar; only now, he was on the couch, lying on his back with his eyes closed. “You need to lower your hips and straighten your arm,” Norm said. From behind, he put his arms around Laura and nestled his cheek against her downy soft hair, the scent of wildflowers in the rain. As he helped her feel a smooth stroke, she brushed her buttock against his upper thigh. Norm jumped back! His eyes made a beeline for the sofa. Dave was out cold!

“Don’t worry about him,” she said, “He just chugged two triple shots of 150 proof, Jamaican rum!”

“That’s weird. He usually drinks me under the table.”

“I gave you single shots of regular Bacardi.”

They chuckled, suddenly paused, then slammed together and necked with reckless abandon! When his pelvis pressed against her belly, she could feel the rumours were true—Norm was indeed enormous! She couldn’t wait to grab hold of his gigantic cock, slid her hand off his tush and around his hip—they jumped apart as if split by lightening, startled half to death by Dave, who’d sat up and was now mumbling. Norm had lipstick smeared all over his mouth. Laura gestured for him to wipe it off. He turned away and used his sleeve.

Dave squinted his vision into focus. “Whoa…Laura…you sure mix a mean drink! Norm…you still here? Go on home. I’m gonna take a nap.” His feet remained planted on the floor as his torso fell sideways upon the sofa. He snored like a buzz saw.

“His tolerance for alcohol is scary!” Norm said. “I have a hard time keeping up with him. Of course, he can handle more booze ‘cause he’s quite a bit bigger than me.”

(*Not where it counts*, she thought.) "We can't leave him, Norm. If he wakes up and finds us alone in another room, *he'd freak!* Do you play chess?"

"I know how to move the pieces, that's about it."

She took his hand and led him to a small table in front of a picture window, along the same wall as the sofa Dave was passed out on. A full moon lit the night sky and reflected upon a chessboard, built into an oak tabletop. After they made several moves, Laura slid her high heel shoe along the parquet floor, out from under the table. The extension of her leg automatically hiked her skirt, as if she wasn't wearing one from Norm's perspective. As his eyes bulged at her long, luscious leg, her queen pinned his knight. "You sure know how to apply the pressure," he said.

She reached down, unbuckled the strap around her ankle and teasingly slid her foot in and out of her shoe. After a long pause, he said, "Uh, whose move is it?" Her answer was to slide her stockinged foot up his leg…along his inner thigh…and across his fat ball sack—she gasped when she realized his shlong was longer than the bottom of her foot and almost as wide! The mere touch of him sent a shockwave through her wet loins, in the throes of her first full-blown orgasm!

The intensity of her release put Norm, himself, on the brink…one more shudder of her grasping toes and…Laura slammed her foot to the floor—Dave was sitting up! He turned to face them. "What are you guys doin' over there?"

Laura stifled her heavy breathing and nodded at the board. "Playing chess." She slipped her foot back into her shoe and hid the unclasped buckle under the table.

"Your sister can really play!" Norm said. "Very aggressive how she moves her men around."

Dave rubbed his eyes. "I don't know what happened. Those drinks hit me like a ton of bricks! What are you guys doing?"

"Chess Dave, we're playing chess," Laura said, "I asked Norm to stay in case I needed help getting you upstairs. You wouldn't want dad to find you passed out down here, would you?"

"Guess not. I'm alright now. I think. Norm, go on home. I'll talk to you tomorrow."

"Okay partner, I'll let myself out." With his back turned to Dave, Norm flashed googly eyes at Laura. Then he left.

Laura buckled her shoe, then caressed her chess pieces while savouring the game she had played. "Ballet in the morning," she suddenly said, "I should go to bed."

"No, wait. Sit with me awhile."

Reluctantly, she joined him on the sofa.

"Did you have a good time, entertaining my friend?" he said.

"Norm's a little boring. No offence. I know he's your best friend and all."

"He sure doesn't measure up to your ol' brother, does he?"

After a paroxysm of laughter, she forced a yawn. "I'm really tired. Goodnight, Dave."

"What's your hurry?" He slid beside her and reached for her knee; she removed his hand instantly. "Dave, don't. We should talk about what happened. What would our parents say? Your dad would kill us both!"

"I don't give a damn what he thinks! We're not really brother and sister. If our parents didn't get married, I definitely would have asked you out."

"But our parents did get married. I don't feel comfortable with anything other than a normal, brother-sister relationship."

"A little late for that NOW!"

Laura cringed at the sudden rage in his piercing, blue eyes.

He took a calming breath. "As you know, I've dated tons of girls. None of them compares to you. You have to admit, I'm not so bad myself. Name someone who's tougher or better looking than I am."

"Dave, I think what we went through in Mexico created a weird bond between us. We need to move past it, get on with our lives."

"You wouldn't have a life if it wasn't for me! Those Mexicans would have gang–banged you, then slit your throat!"

"Reality check, Dave! If it wasn't for you, I wouldn't have been exposed to them in the first place! Remember? You forced me to go."

"Little miss prissy, can't ever be wrong. You think you're so perfect!"

"Whatever, Dave. I'm going to bed."

"Alright, let's do it one last time and I'll never ask again."

"*What? No way—never again*!" She stood up to leave.

"Never say never, bitch!" He grabbed her hips and flipped her face down upon the sofa. With one hand, he held her down by the neck; with his other hand, he yanked up her skirt and tore the crotch out of her nylons. Amid muffled cries, she flailed her fist back, then jabbed her elbow into his abdomen. Her blow didn't affect him whatsoever. He undid his pants and pulled out his rabid cock. Before he could ram it into her, she dug her thick, meticulously kept fingernails into his forearm and clawed out a clump of flesh!

"Fucking bitch!" His blood dripped to the floor like heavy raindrops before a thunderstorm. He lunged to the bar and wrapped a dishtowel around his gash.

Tears had smeared Laura's mascara like a gothic mask. "IT'S OVER BETWEEN US—UNDERSTAND? OVER!"

"It's not over until I say it is! You think you're so much better than me? Look at you, snot pouring from your nose, bawling like a baby." He cackled, then said, "I never noticed it before, but that birthmark on your ass—it's shaped like Texas!"

"You're a monster!"

"Oh, come on now. When we fucked last week, you wanted it as much as I did. Don't go getting so high and mighty on me. We could be good together."

Laura fled to her bedroom, locked the door, then ran a hot bath in her en suite. After stuffing her clothes into a garbage pail, she stepped into the tub and forced herself to sit in the steaming hot water. Sweat mixed with her tears as if her flesh weighed in on her weeping. Faint with heat, she drained the tub and ran a shower. As the cool water soothed her puffy, red skin, she despaired knowing it would take a lot more than a mild scalding to rid herself of the life-sucking leech that was her stepbrother.

Chapter Eight

Slouched upon a sofa in his rec room, Miles stared at the slow, downward swirl of dust, lit by a sliver of twilight, leaking in from a crack between the curtains above his head. Glum for a week now, he'd plummeted from the ecstasy of losing his cherry to Tammy, to the agony of losing Sheila, who ignored him at school as if they'd never met.

The hall light flicked on and Jo skipped down the stairs. He turned on a lamp and said, "Trying to go all *cryptic Poe* on me?"

Miles glanced at his cousin, then looked down at the shag carpet.

"So you're having a hard time getting over Sheila."

"How'd you guess?"

"It's all you've been thinking about since I came out of the hospital."

"Yeah, well, I really miss her."

"But something happened today to make it worse."

"How'd you know?"

"Just a hunch."

"Know that *dink* who stars in the school play?"

"Bob Payne?"

"Yeah, only I call him Bob *Payne-in-the-Ass*. Sheila's been goin' out with him."

"That has to hurt. I have something that might cheer you up." Jo reached inside his jacket and pulled out a mickey of lemon gin.

Miles brightened considerably. "You sure have loosened up since…"

"It's okay Miles, I don't mind talking about it."

"It's just that you seem a lot more easy going these days."

"Indeed, my brush with death has given me a new lease on life."

They went to the bar and Jo poured a couple shots. "Cheers," Miles said. They tossed lemon gin past their gums, then downed two more shots.

"Miles, I don't think you should go to the play tonight."

"How'd you know I was going?"

"Had a hunch."

"I swear, ever since you came out of the hospital, it's like you can read my mind—it's starting to freak me out!"

"I guess it's time I told you about my new gift; but before I do, you have to promise you'll *never-ever* tell anyone."

"So much for easy going! Okay, you have my word."

"You already nailed it: Ever since my recovery from catatonia, I can hear people's thoughts."

"You mean, like, you're a mind reader?"

"Yes, I'm quite clairvoyant."

Miles slammed his shot glass on the bar and burst into laughter. "What do you take me for, some kind of idiot?"

"Think of a number, any number at all."

"Okay, got it."

"Seven thousand, seven hundred and seventy…six. You were going to go with all sevens but felt it was too repetitive, so you changed the last digit to six."

Miles nearly fell off his barstool! "That's amazing! How'd it happen?"

"Who knows? I sense my telepathy as karma, a sort of cosmic compensation for what I went through. Perhaps there's a gift attached to every affliction if one is lucky enough to find it."

"So, 'Whatever doesn't kill you makes you stronger!'"

"Whoa Miles, did you just quote Nietzsche?"

"Oh yeah, me and Nietzsche, we go *waaaay* back!"

Both cousins broke into laughter. They clinked glasses and chugged another shot. "I know what you're thinking Miles, the possibilities seem endless. No, I won't become a professional poker player. I'll work for humanitarian causes after high school. For now, I just want to enjoy what's left of my youth."

"What about the amnesia? Is it true you can't remember who beat you up?"

"No, I lied."

"Who did it then?"

"I can't tell you that."

"Why not? You could go to the police and—"

"Miles! Do you care about my parents?"

"Of course."

"If the authorities find out who assaulted me, my parents will be killed!"

"How do you know that? Can you see into the future as well?"

"No, but one of the assailants threatened to kill my parents if I ever 'squealed on him.' Miles, he meant it. So don't tell anyone I know who assaulted me, okay?"

"You have my word. Too bad though. I'd love to see the *bastard* pay for what he did to you."

"Don't worry, Miles. I've read his thoughts recently—he's on a 'Highway to Hell!'" Jo sipped his gin, then said, "What time are we leaving for the play?"

"You're coming with me?"

"Can I talk you out of going?"

"No."

"Well then, I won't let you go through this alone."

***

At eight o'clock, the two cousins sat in the Perth Bay cafetorium, front row and center. "You might like this play, Miles. *Kiss Me Kate* is a romantic comedy that takes place during a fictional production of Shakespeare's *The Taming of the Shrew*."

"What? Oh. Jo, if my veins weren't so full of adrenaline, I'd fall asleep during the first act!"

"So, your plan is to confront Sheila, explain how it wasn't your fault you slept with her sister, and, if at all possible, punch Bob Payne in the nose!"

"Works for me."

Jo sighed and shook his head.

The curtains parted and the play began. Miles felt his blood boil when Bob Payne entered the stage. *Kiss Me Kate*? he thought, More like *Kiss Me Sheila*!

"You're getting yourself all worked up," Jo whispered, "Try to stay calm."

Miles took a deep breath. His heartbeat had just returned to normal when he spotted Sheila off to the side, watching Bob from behind the bunched-up curtain. As soon as she saw Miles, she ducked out of sight. His inclination was to jump onto the stage and confront her right then and there. He sprung to his feet!

Jo grabbed his arm and pulled him back to his seat. "Miles!" he said in a harsh whisper, "If you make a scene up there, you'll be expelled! Be cool. Wait for the intermission."

People in the audience hushed them. Miles whispered near Jo's ear, "You're right, you're right." He tried to be patient but the first half of the play seemed to drag on for a half century. In real time, the curtains closed after forty minutes.

"I don't believe it," Jo said, "After all *that* you're afraid to confront her?"

"Yeah, well…"

"You know, we can leave right now and forget the whole thing."

"No, this is something I have to do."

"Can I come with you?"

"No Jo, I have to do it on my own."

Jo sighed. "Alright then, I'll be right here if you need me."

Miles slunk to the rear entrance of the stage and asked around for Sheila. One of the prop hands, a guy in coveralls, said she might've gone to the boiler room for a smoke. When Miles walked down the hallway, his knees felt like rubber as his heart pounded erratic beats. He hesitated at the boiler room door. Maybe Jo was right, he thought, maybe I should just leave. But then he heard Sheila moan, "*God, oh God*!"

He quietly opened the door, slipped into the room and peeked around the boiler. There was Sheila, laid upon a table, her ankles up around Bob's ears, his hips pumping her like a jackrabbit!

Miles's first inclination was to grab one of the folded chairs, leaning against the wall, and smash Bob's head! But all his rage channelled south, pooling into a massive erection! The only other time he had watched someone else having sex was when a classmate charged five bucks to see a stag film in his garage. Now, he was watching it live—for real! Although it aroused him like mad, the humiliation was worse than anything his mother had ever done to him. He felt like the epitome of pathetic.

Dazed and teary eyed, he returned to the cafetorium. Even without clairvoyance, Jo would have sensed his cousin's anguish. He stood and put his arm around him. "I'm so sorry you went through that, Miles. Let's get out of here."

As Jo pulled away from the school in his mother's Ford Pinto, he said, "Now Miles, don't think about doing anything rash. Obviously, you're hurting like hell right now; but believe me, you deserve much better than Sheila."

"You've been warning me about her all along. I just wouldn't listen."

"Some things you have to learn for yourself."

"Jo, thanks for being patient. Thanks for being there."

"It's the least I could do Pal, especially after all the time you spent visiting me in the hospital." Jo realized there wasn't much else he could say to lift his cousin's spirits. Instead, he envisioned a series of events that would erase Sheila Babcock from his cousin's thoughts, as if he'd never known her.

Chapter Nine

Saturday morning, Miles assumed his position, slouched on the sofa in his dim, dank rec room. The image of Sheila with her ankles around Bob's ears flashed through his thoughts like a projector on a hellish loop, gripping his heart like a devil's claw. Jo came down the stairs and flicked the light on beside the sofa. "Second day in a row I've found you down here brooding. Do you want to talk about it?"

"How could she do this to me? What does Bob *Payne-In-the-Ass* have that I don't? He doesn't love her the way I do—I would die for her—in fact, that's what I'm doing right now, dying for her little by little! I was such an idiot to think she'd ever—"

"Alright Miles, I get it: Life's a bitch and then you die!"

Miles glared at his cousin.

"Don't give me that look—I'm here to help you! Go grab your gym bag."

"What for?"

"So we can go shoot hoops at the Y."

"There's no point. I'm gonna quit the basketball team."

"What? You love basketball."

"I'm tired of sitting on the bench, and sick to death of the pranks my teammates play on me."

Jo dashed to the garage and grabbed a basketball. When he returned to the rec room, Miles was lying with his forearm laid across his eyes like a blindfold.

"Here, catch," Jo said.

Miles peeked under his arm. "I'm not into it."

Jo stepped up to the sofa, lifted the ball shoulder height, then dropped it on his cousin's stomach! Miles convulsed. "WHAT'D YA DO THAT FOR?"

"Come on, Pal. You need to forget about Sheila for a while. Let's go play."

"Do you have a hearing problem?"

Jo snatched the ball off the floor and said, "I'll pass it to you, ready?"

He lobbed the ball to Miles….who swatted it away, into a lamp, which fell to the floor and smashed to pieces. Betty charged down the stairs. "MY LAMP! MY LAMP! HOW MANY TIMES HAVE I TOLD YOU? DON"T PLAY WITH YOUR BALLS IN THE HOUSE!"

Miles sat up. "SORRY ABOUT YOUR DAMN LAMP!"

Betty was shocked. It was the first time he had yelled back at her.

He took a deep breath. "Sorry, mom. It was an accident."

"Okay. Accidents happen. I guess." She looked at her nephew. "You're looking much better Jo."

"Thanks, aunt Betty. Have you lost weight?"

"As a matter of fact, I lost five pounds."

Miles rolled his eyes. "We're going to play basketball, mom. See ya."

"You boys have a good time."

As the cousins climbed into the orange Pinto, Jo sensed a wave of anguish flooding his cousin's heart. He started the car and said, "Hey Miles, did you catch what your mother said when she saw the broken lamp?"

“What? Oh yeah, she told me *I shouldn’t play with my balls in the house*!”

They burst into laughter. Jo kept the conversation light for the entire drive. Before Miles knew it, they were pulling into the parking lot of the Y.M.C.A. Both cousins paid the nominal fee, then headed for the change room. While they slipped into their shorts, Jo said, “So what’s the best way for you to train?”

“Well, the coach rarely lets me work on my shot. I’m always playing defence against the starters.”

“Alright, then. I’ll play D, so you can work on your shot.”

The gym was busy, but equipped with six baskets. The cousins claimed the last available hoop. Jo fed crisp passes to Miles, who sunk the majority of his shots; but then Sheila crept into his thoughts, and his aim went awry. Sensing her presence, Jo fired a pass at Miles—then ran right into him!

“What t’ hell?” Miles said, upon his butt, looking up from the floor, “There’s no body checking in basketball!”

“What’s the matter? Can’t play tough?”

“Alright, if you want to play tough, how about a little one on one?”

“Bring it on Coz, bring it on!”

Miles took first possession. He faked left, tore to the right and skied himself for a jump shot—Swish!

“Great shot, Miles!”

On defence, Miles eased up, letting his cousin score the odd basket; on offence, he dominated, his typical shot like the end of a rainbow crashing through the net.

An hour and a half later, Jo said, “That’s it for me—I’m pooped!”

Miles smiled at his cousin. "Thanks Jo, you were right. This was a lot better than moping around the house all day."

"No problem, Pal."

They raided the water fountain, then headed for the sauna. Jo inhaled the soothing scent of cedar. "So, you're not quitting the basketball team, right?"

"I guess not; though, I'm tired of the pranks they play on me. Did I tell you someone peed in my shampoo bottle last week?"

"That's brutal. Maybe it's time you stood up for yourself."

Miles agreed. Then Jo sensed Sheila joining them in the sauna.

"Sorry Jo, I can't stop thinking about her!"

"Fret not my friend—for tonight, we shall set you free!"

***

Jo returned to his cousin's house that evening after dinner.

"What's in the bags?" Miles asked.

"I bought you some clothes. Come on, let's go to your room."

Once they were in the bedroom, Miles opened one of the parcels and found a navy-blue, button-up shirt. He tried it on and held out his arms. "The sleeves are long enough! I love it, Jo—thanks!"

Jo handed his cousin a pair of black shoes, dressier than running shoes, yet casual enough to wear with jeans.

"They're cool Jo, but these are size twelve; I wear size nine."

Jo chuckled. "They're supposed to be too big."

"I don't follow."

"Your main problem with girls is that you get too tense, right?"

"Yeah, probably. How are these clodhoppers gonna help?"

"They'll feel funny when you walk, like you're wearing clown shoes, a constant reminder to stay loose, so you won't take yourself too seriously."

"You might be onto something, it's making me laugh just thinking about it! Still, I'm not wearing oversized shoes unless you are."

"My size twelve's are parked in the front hall. Pack some tissue into the toes and lace them up. We have to go. It's Saturday, there's bound to be a line-up."

***

Jo parked his mother's Pinto in front of a bar called Night 'N Gales. Miles said, "Have you been here before?"

"No, but there's a dorm for student nurses less than a kilometre away."

"What a great strategy for meeting chicks! But how do we get in without IDs?"

"Leave that to me."

After several groups of female students paid admittance and entered the bar, the cousins stood before the doorman. The burly fellow said, "Can I see your—"

"Isn't that your 67' Camaro over there?" Jo said, pointing across the street.

The doorman's chest came out a little. "How'd you know—"

"That was the first year Chevy came out with that model, right?"

"Yeah, it's the only year they put vent windows in the doors. Funny, I was just thinking about how lucky I was to find one."

"That's the coolest car I've ever seen," Miles said, catching on to what his cousin was doing. "You keep that baby in mint condition!"

"Thanks." The doorman looked over their shoulders and saw a group of five young ladies getting impatient. "There's a three dollar cover charge, fellas."

Jo paid him six bucks and the Martini cousins entered the bar. As they walked to the coat check, Miles started to laugh. "These shoes—I can't stop scuffing my heels!"

"At least you're not walking like an old man! I'm so stiff from playing basketball, it feels like knives going into my thighs every time I take a step!"

After checking their coats, the cousins schlepped passed a dance floor, loaded with gyrating young women, lit intermittently by a strobe light. "Heart of Glass" blasted from the stereo. As Miles perched upon a barstool, he said, "The girl to guy ratio in here is amazing—must be five chicks to every guy!"

"Some of these young ladies have been checking us out already."

Miles grinned from ear to ear. A full figured bartender approached. Before she could ask for IDs, Jo said, "Do you ever get a night off?"

"What do you mean?

"You were working the night my sister brought me here for a birthday beer."

"That was nice of her. Happy birthday. Can't say I remember you, though."

"I remember you because, well, who could forget your gorgeous green eyes?"

"Thanks," she said, smiling and blushing. "What can I get you boys?"

"Two Export Ales, please," Miles said.

The barkeep set two brewskies before them. "That'll be $3.50."

"I got it Jo, you paid the cover." He paid alright—*the exact amount*! Jo chipped in a tip before she could walk away.

"Damn, I forgot the tip! Sorry Jo. How can you tell it's my first time in a bar?"

"That's okay Pal, I've got your back." They clinked bottles together and swigged ice cold beer. "You look great in that shirt, Miles."

"Thanks. You're a lifesaver. I rarely have anything decent to wear."

"Miles, why don't you get a job so you can buy your own clothes?"

"My dad says I don't need to rush it, because once I start working, I'll be doing it the rest of my life."

Jo sensed the conversation was making his cousin feel uneasy, so he changed gears. "Miles, it's time for you to go to the washroom."

"But I don't have to go yet."

"Just go through the motions. Trust me."

Miles clod-hopped to the washroom. When he returned to the bar, Jo said to him, "See the redhead, sitting at the table, left of the dance floor?"

"You mean the chick who's way out my league?"

"She thought you were 'cute' when you walked by."

"Get out. You've got to be kidding!"

"I kid you not. This is what you can say to her…" Jo leaned close to his cousin and whispered.

After listening intently, Miles said, "Are you sure about all that stuff?"

"Trust me, it's all true."

Miles chugged the rest of his beer, then shuffled across the bar, his oversized shoes like two ocean liners on a parallel course. He knelt beside the young red head and said, “Cindy DaSilva, from Saskatoon, right?”

She smiled, but furrowed her brows. “Do I know you?”

“You were a couple grades ahead of me, but we took the same school bus. You had a tire hanging from a tree, in your front yard, right?”

“I’ll be darned, someone from my home town!” She gave him a big hug.

Empowered by her embrace, he said, “When I was little, I thought you were pretty; but now you’re downright gorgeous!”

“That’s sweet.” She kissed him on the cheek. The D.J played “How Deep is Your Love.” She asked Miles to dance. Normally, he would have declined. But it was a slow song and he longed to be close to her.

Entwined, they swayed. The scent of her lilac shampoo made him unsteady… he stepped on her toes twice! “Sorry about that,” he said.

She looked down. “No wonder you’re having trouble: look at the size of your feet!” She seemed mesmerized. “You know what they say about big feet, don’t you?”

Miles gave her a quizzical look. “No, what do *they* say?”

“Don’t worry. It’s not a bad thing.”

When the song ended, she took his hand and led him back to her table. Jo was already sitting there with her friend, an attractive young woman with black, curly hair.

“Miles, I’d like you to meet Kelly.”

Miles thought she looked a little like Cher. He smiled, shook her hand, then introduced Cindy to Jo. A waitress served a tray of B52 shooters. Jo paid for the drinks, then raised his glass: "Here's to new friends!"

They each downed a shooter. The song "Brick House" blared through the bar. The girls pulled the cousins onto the dance floor. Miles panicked! Jo said, "Don't worry, I'll help you."

Enthralled by the funky music, the young women shook and shimmied, Cindy in a flirty denim skirt, Kelly in a tight pair of faded Levi's.

Jo said to his cousin, "Start with something simple, like this:" He moved his left knee and shoulder forward for two beats, then did the same with his right side. Almost instantly, Miles was able to mimic Jo in sync with the music. "Okay, looks good, Miles. Now move your hips and arms like you're downhill skiing."

It worked! Miles skied to the beat. Jo said, "Now move as if you're paddling a canoe, two strokes on each side of the boat."

Miles stroked an imaginary paddle twice to his right then to his left. Jo said, "Now improvise moves between the skiing and canoeing."

"Thanks Jo, this is fun!"

The girls stepped up to the Martinis, twisted to the floor, then wiggled back up to their feet. It was the cousins' turn to go down, only Jo's thighs were so sore, he couldn't get back up! Miles gave him a hand. Both cousins cracked up laughing.

The four of them put an arm around each other, forming a circle. Jo planted a kiss on Kelly's lips. Cindy kissed Miles. They returned to the table and Miles proposed a toast: "Here's to my grandparents who go drinkin' and dancin' at the Slovenian Club in Europe!"

Jo smiled, knowing that the girls thought it was sweet Miles had toasted his grandparents. They all tossed back another shot.

Drinking and dancing—dancing and drinking, they were having so much fun, the night seemed to fly by in an instant. Miles couldn't believe it when last call was announced. The girls whispered back and forth, then Kelly said, "Would you guys like to join us for a nightcap, at our apartment?"

Miles's eyes lit up like two bright blue stars! Jo said to the girls, "Sure, we'd love to." He knew better than to drink and drive, so he called a cab. Outside, the foursome was greeted by a fresh sheet of snow. "Snowball fight!" Jo declared. They split into teams, boys against the girls. After several lobs at each other, Jo said, "Come on Miles, ATTACK!"

Though Miles and Jo were pelted with snow, they tackled the girls upon a lawn, and wrestled them in jest. Jo brushed his chin against Kelly's neck, between her clinched shoulder and jaw, making her laugh so hard, he had to back off so she could catch her breath! Meanwhile, Cindy washed Miles's face out with snow. In retaliation, he slipped his hands under her blue, bubble jacket and tickled her ribs till she warned him she was going to pee if he didn't stop!

"Cab's here," Jo suddenly said. He sat in the front seat. Miles sat in the back, between the two girls. He started necking with Cindy and was shocked when Kelly rested her hand upon his thigh.

They reached the nearby high-rise and Miles spent his last dollars paying for their ride. The lip locking foursome grew handsy in the elevator with a squeeze of buttock here, a brush of breast there, all of them flushed with arousal by the time they entered the girl's suite.

"Nice place," Jo said. Oil paintings of Greek gods and goddesses surrounded burgundy walls. A huge, bearskin rug lay before a fireplace. Jo followed Kelly into the kitchen while Miles helped Cindy build a fire.

Before long, a flame spiked and crackled from the crow's nest of kindling. Cindy added a couple of split logs. Kelly returned with a tray, carting four glasses of white wine. Jo carried a serving plate with sliced fruit and cheese. The girls excused themselves to change. *Jo took off his pants*!

"What to hell are you doing?" Miles said, "Have you gone mad?"

"They won't mind. Might as well get comfortable. Trust me."

Reluctantly, Miles stripped down to his skivvies. When the girls returned, his eyes nearly popped out of his head! Each young woman wore a silky camisole. Cindy's was peach with lacy, off-white trim. Kelly's was powder blue, an electric contrast to her raven-black hair. They all sat around the bearskin rug before the roaring fire.

Cindy sipped from her glass, kissed Miles and flooded his mouth with wine. They savoured the taste while French kissing. As Jo kissed Kelly's neck, he chuckled inside and thought, *Ding dong, the Witch is dead—no more Sheila in his head!*

***

Jo lifted Kelly's arm off Miles and gave him a gentle shake. "Wake up, Pal."

Miles opened his eyes and stretched. "What time is it?"

"Four-fifteen." A few red embers was all that remained of the fire.

"Good thing I'm sleeping at your house. Betty'd have a bird if I came home this late!"

"Come on, I've already called a cab."

Miles pulled his clothes on, then kissed both girls on the cheek, careful to not awaken them. On the elevator, he was bouncing on his heels.

Jo said, “I know—what a night!”

“Older women rock!” Miles said.

“They certainly know what goes where and why.”

After a taxi ride to the bar, the two cousins jumped into the orange Pinto and pulled out of the parking lot. “If it wasn’t for your gift,” Miles said, “I never would’ve had the courage to approach Cindy, never would’ve guessed she liked the look of me, not in a million years!”

Jo started to laugh.

“What’s so funny?”

“I have a confession to make, but you have to promise you won’t get mad.”

“Alright, I promise. What is it?”

“It’s just that Cindy didn’t notice you at all, not until you approached her brimming with confidence.”

“Son-of-a-bee!”

“I’m sorry for lying, but—”

“Save it Jo. This is the best night of my life! If I live to be a hundred, I still won’t be able to thank you enough.”

“What are good cousins for, Miles, what are we for?”

Chapter Ten

"Stop, STOP IT—AHHH!" Norm Pattison awoke in a cold sweat.

His mother rushed into his room. "Are you alright dear?"

"I had a bad dream."

"You've been having a lot of those lately."

"I'm fine, mom. Goodnight."

"Goodnight, dear."

She closed the door and went back to bed. Minutes later, Norm slinked through the house like a cat burglar. He opened the liquor cabinet, then swigged mouthfuls of vodka. He didn't have to be Freud to figure out his nightmares. They all ended the same way, with his eye socket punctured by the pointy toe of Dave's cowboy boot!

He replaced the bottle, then staggered back to his room. Despite the dampening affect of booze, he couldn't fall back asleep. Laura's plan had exacerbated his angst. Since her parents were leaving for a four day weekend at their condo in Mexico, she thought it would be a perfect opportunity for her and Norm to steal away, to her family's cottage north of Kingston.

As he watched the second hand circle his alarm clock, Dutch courage kicked in. A weekend alone with Laura—to hell with Dave! he thought, It's time I stood up to him. But not till after the weekend.

***

Tucking books into his locker for lunch hour, Norm felt like he could fall asleep like a horse, standing on his feet. The prickly stress of his secret relationship would soon be worth it, his getaway with Laura a mere afternoon away. In the middle of a massive yawn, his locker door slammed against his shoulder. "Jesus Dave—what'd ya do that for?"

"What's the matter—wrong time of the month?"

"You caught me off guard is all."

"Wanna play pool tomorrow, before we work out?"

"Can't make it. Have to go to Brockville for my cousin's christening."

"You never mentioned that before."

"I tried to get out of it but mom's making me go."

"Always knew you were a Mamma's boy!" Dave punched him in the shoulder so hard, Norm staggered into his neighbour's locker. "See you in the caf, Pattison."

Meet Dave for lunch? No way—not when all Norm could think about was sinking his huge sausage into Laura, again and again, all weekend long! He went to the library and slept in a study carrel.

Earlier that day, Laura had fabricated a story of her own, telling her brother she'd be gone for the weekend, on a ski trip with Valerie Doberman.

***

At 4:30, Norm drove his mother's Cutlass to Valerie's house. Laura came outside to greet him. "I'd kiss you," she said, "but someone might see us."

"That's okay, we have plenty of time for that when we get to the cottage."

While he loaded her suitcase and supplies into the trunk, Laura said to Valerie, "Have fun skiing with your dad."

"I will. And don't worry, Laura. Your secret's safe with me." When the two friends embraced, Valerie thought, *Lucky Bitch*! She couldn't help feeling envious. After all, she was the one who had dubbed him "Enormous Norm," back when they were dating, less than a year ago.

Laura and Norm jumped into the car and headed north. As he reached across her knees, she thought he'd cop a feel of her stockinged thigh; instead, he popped the glove box open and grabbed a mickey of Canadian Club whisky. She was disappointed he didn't touch her. And now, both his hands were occupied, one with the steering wheel, the other with the bottle. He swilled whisky, then said, "What's your brother up to?"

"Going to a hockey game with my uncle."

"Good. That'll keep him occupied. I don't think he has a clue about us yet."

"We've been careful—we have to be—he'd go *ballistic*!"

By the time they passed the city limits, Norm was half way through the mickey. "How rude of me," he said, "would you like a drink?"

"No thanks. I don't need it." She slid over and opened his pants. As his penis took life in her hand, the sun set beneath the tree tops. When he let go of the wheel and pulled the headlights on, tires on the passenger side dipped onto the gravel shoulder. He grabbed the wheel and veered back onto the road. "You're makin'n it *hard*...to concentrate."

"Poor baby! Want me to stop?" ("No!") When she went down on him, her magnificent hair covered his lap like a silken tent.

He savoured her eager mouth by moaning and briefly closing his eyes…when he looked at the road again, a fawn stood frozen by his headlights! As Norm swerved left and hit the brakes, his bumper clipped the animal's jaw. The car hit a patch of ice and slid sideways down the highway. Tires on the driver side gained air, but dropped back to the pavement, barely holding the road without rolling the car. The Cutlass came to a stop facing the forest, parked across the left lane like a roadblock.

With a white knuckled grip on wheel, Norm sat frozen in shock. Laura's head popped up. "What happened?" She wiped spittle from the corner of her mouth.

"We hit a small deer." He swigged whiskey, then backed up to the dead animal.

"What are you doing?"

"I should remove the carcass before someone else crashes into it."

"Aren't there workmen for that sort of thing?"

"It'll only take a minute." They both got out of the car. "It's a young male," he said, grabbing the buck by its hind legs and dragging it off the highway. Its head was limp with a broken neck. Norm squatted and stroked fur above its ear.

Laura set her hand upon Norm's shoulder. "Animals jump in front of cars all the time. There was nothing you could have done about it."

Norm inspected his mother's car. The right headlight was smashed to pieces, the front right fender was buckled. Laura said, "Will you get into trouble for that?"

"Nah. My dad owns an insurance company. He'll find a way to cover it."

For the rest of the ride, they listened to the radio and barely uttered a word. By the time they reached the log cabin, Norm had polished off the entire mickey. He didn't stop soon enough at the end of the driveway and bashed into a tree.

“Damn it, Norm! We’re lucky to make it here alive!” She took a deep, calming breath. “The bottle’s empty, you’re done drinking, right?”

“*Do you beautiful you are, ya know*?” He set his head back and closed his eyes.

Perhaps a nap would sober him up. She made trips lugging luggage and supplies into the cottage. It was cold inside, but the cabin was winterized, fully insulated. She turned the furnace on and lit a fire in the woodstove. When she finished putting the groceries away, she grabbed a flashlight and went outside. But Norm wasn’t in the car. A branch snapped in the darkness. She scanned the forest with her flashlight. “Norm! What are you doing there?” He lay face down in a bush.

“Hey? Oh, I had to pee. Got tangled in these branches.”

Great! she thought. She helped him to his feet, slung his arm over her shoulder and walked him into the cottage. He went straight to his gym bag and grabbed a twenty-sixer of Smirnoff vodka. “Have any mix, Laura?”

“Don’t you think you’ve had enough for now?”

“Forget it. I can drink it straight.”

“Good God! Hold on, I’ll get you some mix.”

Laura went to the pantry and found a bottle of flat cola. Norm mixed himself a stiff drink. “Can I pour you one?” he asked.

“I already told you, I don’t need it.” She added a log to the crackling fire, then sat beside him on a sofa. His head oscillated. She slid the drink out of his hand and set it on an end table. “You’re not going to pass out on me again, are you?”

“Would I that do?” he slurred. “Been dreaming about this forever!”

"Let's not waste time then." She jumped up, lifted his ankle between her legs, pried one of his boots off, then the other. After she undid his jeans, he lifted his hips, and when she yanked his pants off, she nearly tugged him right off the sofa! His high pitched, hyena's laugh neither impressed her, nor deterred her. She lifted her skirt and tore a hole in the crotch of her nylons. But he was limp. And dozing off again. "Norm—wake up!"

"Huh? I'm awake, I'm awake!"

She stroked his penis until it was at half-mast, then straddled him, a partial erection plenty long enough to penetrate her. He tipped to the side. Laura propped him up. "Norm…stay awake—*PLEASE*!"

"What? I'm awake, I'm…ZZZ."

She slapped his face and ground her hips, about to gush all over him when his limp dick slipped out of her! She inserted two of his fingers and salvaged a fraction of the orgasm she had been denied. His mouth popped open amid snoring. She covered him with a blanket, then spent the night reading outdated fashion magazines.

Just before ten, Norm bolted to the washroom and heaved his guts out. He slumped back to her and said, "Don't know why I drank so much. I've ruined our first night together."

"It's alright, we have the whole weekend." She gave him two Aspirins and a glass of water.

"I promise to make it up to you."

"Darn right you will, Buster!"

They went to bed and Norm fell asleep with his head on her shoulder. As Laura stroked his hair, it surprised her how much she enjoyed taking care of him.

***

The next morning, Norm awoke to the smell of sizzling bacon. He found Laura in the kitchen, cooking up a storm.

"Good morning," she said, "Feeling better?"

"Yes, thank you. Haven't slept that well for a long time."

She started him off with coffee and orange juice. He downed all the juice. "Thirsty much?" she said.

"You'd think drinking all that booze would make a person *less* thirsty; but it's just the opposite."

She served breakfast. "This is pretty good, Laura."

"Thanks. It reminds me of when I used to play house with our cook."

"I like playing house with you. It sure beats sneaking around. I'm getting tired of all that cloak and dagger stuff. Isn't it time we told your brother about us?"

Laura froze with a fork full of scrambled eggs above her plate. "We're not telling him—*he'd go berserk*!"

"He's more like a jealous husband than a brother, isn't he?"

"Let's not waste the weekend worrying about Dave."

"You're right. He'll find out about us sooner or later anyway. I think he already suspects something."

"What makes you say that?"

"It's not easy to hide how I feel about you."

"Then you have to be more careful! You have no idea what he's capable of."

Norm sipped some coffee, then bolted to the washroom.

Something told Laura she wasn't done nursing him yet.

***

Before playing pool, Dave stepped into a convenience store and bought a pack of wine-tipped cigars. A woman behind him said, “Your father likes to smoke those.”

Dave turned around. “*Mrs. Doberman*?”

“Are you okay? I didn’t mean to startle you, Dave.”

“It’s just that, I thought you were at Mont Tremblant, skiing.”

“Gosh no. I hate the cold. Valerie and her father go every year without me.”

“Oh,” Dave said, relaxing his posture. “So the three of them went?”

“Three? I’m not sure what you mean.”

“Laura went with Valerie, right?”

“Not that I’m aware of. I’m sure Val would’ve mentioned it if Laura was tagging along.”

Without another word, he stormed out of the store.

***

Late Sunday evening, Norm dropped Laura off at Valerie Doberman’s house. Valerie then borrowed her father’s car to drive Laura home. The raven haired beauty was giddy and braggadocio about her sex-filled weekend with Enormous Norm. When the car stopped in front of the Needler mansion, Laura said, “Don’t forget: not a word of this to anyone. I mean it Val. I’m trusting you with my life!”

“*Your life*? I don’t understand all the drama but don’t worry, your secret is safe with me.”

Laura pulled her luggage out of the car, waved good-bye to her friend, then went inside. She set her suitcase in the foyer and flicked a light switch. “JESUS, DAVE—you scared me half to death! What are you doing, sitting there in the dark?”

Dave sipped from a cocktail glass. “How was skiing?”

“Great—we had eleven inches of powder! Exhausting though, all that fresh air and exercise. I’m going straight to bed.” She took a step up the stairs.

“STRAIGHT TO HELL—THAT’S WHERE THE TWO OF YOU ARE GOING—STRAIGHT TO HELL!”

Laura froze. “What are you talking about?”

“*Fucked anyone lately*?”

She dashed to her room, locked the door, then sat on her bed, shaking. There was a clicking sound at her door, then a pop. After picking her lock with a paperclip, Dave barged in and stood before her. “Don’t you want to know how I found out?”

“I don’t care. My private life is none of your business!”

“I bumped into Mrs. Doberman. Once I knew you weren’t skiing, the rest was easy to figure out. You and Norm are stinkin’ liars! I should have known. For weeks now, he’s had a *stupid*, silly grin on his face, whenever you’re around. So where’d you shack up?”

“None of your business!”

“SO YOU ADMIT IT—you *did* shack up with him!”

“Why are you doing this?”

“He’s my best friend. I have a right to know.”

“Like hell you do—get out of my room!”

“Just tell me if you fucked him or not, and I’ll go.”

“Alright, YES—I fucked him all weekend long! And guess what? He has a *huge dick*, much bigger than yours!”

Dave smashed her mouth with the back of his hand, knocking her flat upon the bed. He jumped on top of her and grabbed her wrists.

"What's the matter?" she said, "Can't get it up? Keep telling yourself—*size doesn't matter—be thankful for the little things in life*!" She laughed hysterically.

Seething, his eyes went maniacal and buggy as he seemed to stare through her.

"What were you thinking, Dave? That we'd live in this house together, forever? HEY—snap out of it! You're hurting my wrists—get off me!"

She squirmed, but he was much too heavy and strong for her. "You're no better than those creeps in Mexico—**HELP, RAPE**!"

There was a knock on her open door and Martha, their house servant, said, "Are you alright Laura?"

"I don't know. Am I alright *brother dear*?"

He climbed off her, then marched out of her room.

"Should I call your parents, Miss?"

"No, please don't. I'll speak to them when they get home from Mexico." (That's all she needed, Dave Sr. finding out!) "Thanks Martha, that'll be all."

Laura slid a dresser against her door, then collapsed upon her bed. Her wrists were bruised, her lip was swollen; but it was her heart that hurt most. As long as Dave is alive, she thought, he'll be a nightmare from which I'll never awaken. *As long as he is alive*.

Chapter Eleven

Miles knew his teammates had been up to no good because they couldn't hold back their snickering. What prank was it this time? Did someone pee in his shampoo bottle again? He spun the cap off and took a whiff…no acrid scent of urine. He looked at his clothes. Nothing stolen. Then he spotted it: a chalky substance in his athletic supporter.

He took his gym bag into a toilet stall, slipped into his shorts, then burst out of the stall, holding his genitals, "MY BALLS—MY BALLS ARE ON FIRE!"

While his teammates howled with laughter, Miles dashed back into the stall and came out with the contaminated jock dangling on his middle finger. "Which one of you gutless wonders put itching powder in my gear?" (Everyone stopped laughing.) "So whoever did this, doesn't have the guts to face me?" A few guys glanced at a teammate, who kept his eyes fixed on the floor. Miles stepped up to Art Hornbeak and said, "How would you like to *eat* this?"

Art stood up. "Who's gonna make me?"

Miles threw the jock at him: when Art flinched, Miles punched him in the nose and blood gushed forth. "YOU BASTARD!" Art said, pinching his nostrils together on his way to the washroom.

Coach O'Reilly ducked his head into the change room. "What are you *blockheads* waiting for? Christmas? Last one in the gym runs extra laps!"

The practice began with suicide sprints. Teammates kept staring at Miles in disbelief. When Art entered the gym, O'Reilly blasted him for being late. With blood crusting on his T-shirt, he ran punitive laps while the rest of the team broke into scrimmage.

For the first time since making the team, Miles received passes on a regular basis. And he was red hot, nailing his first three jump shots! In his own end, he played his typical don't-give-an-inch defence. Indeed, everything went swimmingly for him until he took his fourth shot, and Tate Cooke reached in and clawed across his eyes! The coach didn't call a foul. He knew what was going on. Miles was threatening to win some of Tate's playing time; they were fighting for rank on the team.

On defence, Miles covered Tate like a second skin. They ended up latching onto a loose ball. Amid a fierce tug-of-war, Miles stopped pulling on the ball and rammed it into Tate's stomach, knocking the wind out of him! Miles then fired a pass to a fast breaking forward, who dribbled to the net for an easy lay up.

By the end of the practice, Miles knew he'd be spending less time on the bench during their next game. Though he was thrilled, he didn't want to seem cocky. After peeling off his clothes, however, he stepped into the shower area with a discernible strut.

***

Later that day, Miles played one-on-one with his cousin, at the Y.M.C.A. He blew by Jo for a lay-up. On the next play, Miles stole the ball, dribbled back to the foul line, turned and nailed a jump shot. Before long, the score was ten-nothing.

"Hey Jo, you're allowed to move your feet if you want to."

"Sorry, Pal. I'm not into it today. I'll just pass you the ball so you can work on your shot."

An hour later, the two cousins rinsed off in the shower, then sat in the sauna.

"No wonder you couldn't play today, Jo: Too much poon-tang—you're becoming a real Casanova!"

"It's true, I've been dating a lot. My gift has given me a lust for life. It has also led me to some interesting insights."

"Like?"

"Well, it surprises me how often people deny their true feelings. Take my mom for instance. It was her birthday on Wednesday. I asked to be excused, shortly after dinner. Had a date waiting. Mom said, 'Go ahead dear, have a nice time.' Meanwhile she was thinking, *He doesn't have time for me anymore.* She was dying inside!"

"Let me guess: you gave her a big hug and stayed."

"What else could I do?"

Miles filled a cup with water and dumped it onto the heater rocks, sizzling an influx of steam. "What else can you tell me about women; I mean, other than stuff about your mom?"

"I can tell you about a girl I met at the mall."

"You picked up a chick at the mall? Cool! What happened?"

"She was sitting at the food court, drinking a soda. Petite figure, feathery blond hair, I thought she was cute. When I walked near her, I sensed she'd be receptive."

"That must be half the battle, knowing if the girl's interested in the first place. There's never any risk of rejection."

"It's true. I don't waste time on a girl if she has negative thoughts about me."

"So then what happened?"

"I sat at a table next to hers and asked if Supertramp was her favourite band."

"You read her mind?"

"No. I saw the album sticking out of her shopping bag."

"Nice ice breaking."

"Thanks. We introduced ourselves. Her name was Janet. We chatted about school, then our families. I mentioned I didn't have a clue what to buy my mother for her birthday. Janet offered to help me shop. She picked out a gold amulet for mom's charm bracelet. In return, I offered to take her to a movie."

"Smooth move, Jo. You made the date seem like you were paying her back for helping you shop, something she probably liked to do in the first place! So you went out with her?"

"Picked her up that night. Since I already knew she liked Supertramp, I played *Crime of the Century* on my mom's cassette deck. Of course she loved it. But then images of her abusive father spoiled her mood. I diverted her negative thoughts with two words: Cool boots. She perked up instantly, told me where she bought them, how much they cost, why she chose the fawny color instead of black and why she loved that particular leather. I didn't get another word in until we reached the theatre."

"You lured her thoughts to a happier place—brilliant!"

"Indeed, girls sure have a thing for footwear. Anyway, Janet liked horror movies, so I took her to see *Halloween,* a flick about a serial killer named Mike Myers. Well into the movie, a young couple about our age make out on a sofa. The camera pans back revealing the maniac, standing with his back against a wall, cloaked by a shadow.

The scene turned Janet on like crazy! I kissed her and she thought, *Go for my neck, please, suck on my neck!*"

"What an advantage—you had the inside scoop to one of her hot spots!"

"True, but then she surprised me later in the car. We were parked out by the quarry and when I kissed her neck, she pushed me away and ordered me to drive her home—even though I sensed a beautiful warmth spreading throughout her body!"

"Why'd she turn on you like that?"

"Addled thoughts of her father terrified Janet, as if he were in the car with us, cloaked by a shadow, like maniac Mike Myers from the movie."

"Will you see her again?"

"Well, when I dropped her off, she said she'd pay the next time we went out, but I'm not going to call her again. She's too volatile. Besides, I've already moved on."

"Moved on? Wait a minute: this is why you couldn't concentrate when we played today. You've met someone special, haven't you?"

"To be honest, I've embarked upon a relationship that's quite taboo, a lifestyle that would shock and outrage much of society."

"Alright Jo, what's going on?"

"You my friend, will find out soon enough. Man, it's hot in here. I have to get out." Jo jumped off the cedar bench and zipped out of the sauna.

Miles worried about his cousin. The last time Jo was secretive about his love life, he ended up suffering the bizarre rigor of a catatonic stupor.

Chapter Twelve

On a moonless Monday night, Norm parked his mother's banged-up Oldsmobile at a secluded quarry, north of Kingston. He let the engine idle so he could run the heater. "Alright Laura, nobody followed us. What is it you have to tell me?"

"Dave bumped into Valerie's mother on the weekend—*he knows about us*!"

Norm sipped from his mickey. "Good! I'm tired of sneaking around. It's about time he cut you some slack!"

"There's something else." She swallowed a lump in her throat.

"For God sakes Laura, what is it?"

"Dave threatened to spread lies about me."

"What kind of lies?"

"Ugly, grotesque lies about me sleeping with him."

"That's it—*I'm gonna kill him*!" Norm took a swig. "It isn't true is it?"

She slapped his shoulder. "Of course not!"

Her extreme look of disgust convinced him she was telling the truth. "I'm sorry," he said, "it's just that, I never understood why he was so insanely protective of you." He considered telling her about Jo Martini's beating but decided it would only complicate matters.

"What you said earlier...could be our only hope," she said.

"What did I say?"

"You said you were gonna kill him!"

Norm took another belt. "Besides freeing us up to be together, I honestly believe the world would be a better place without him."

She stroked his enormous cock and kissed him as if he were heading off to war. Norm suddenly pulled away from her. "I know how we could get away with it! He likes to point his rifle at your servants—scares the crap out of them when they walk by! It'd be easy to make it look like he had an accident because several witnesses, including myself, would tell the cops about him playing with his gun in the house."

Laura felt her nightmare dissolving with his words. She undid his jeans and went down on him. In a panicked whisper, he said, "Hold on, stop!"

"What is it?"

"SHHH...Did you hear that?"

"No, what—"

"Somebody's out there."

"Let's get out of here!" she said.

He zipped up and sped away from the quarry.

"I want you to know," she said, "our weekend at the cottage meant a lot to me. I'd love it if we could be together like that permanently."

He glanced at her. "You mean, like, get married, and all that?"

"Would that be so terrible?"

"No, not at all. I'd love to marry you. Eventually. After the dust settles."

By the time they reached her house, they had a plan set for Saturday: *Laura would hide Dave's rifle in the storage closet, beside the games room. She'd sneak Norm into the house and he'd hide with the gun. She'd then pretend to make amends with Dave. As a peace offering, she'd make her potent rum punch. When he passed out in the games room, BAM! Laura recommended shooting him under the chin when feigning a self-inflicted wound.*

Norm parked in an alley behind the Needler's mansion. He walked Laura along a cedar hedge. "This is far enough," she said. He kissed her goodnight, then watched her sneak into the house through the servants' entrance.

On his way back to the car, Norm thought he saw a shadow move in the hedge. From a gap in the cedars, Dave materialized like a ghostly demon. He leaned his shoulder against a hydro pole and slipped his hands into the pockets of his football jacket.

"Duh-Dave. What are you doing here?"

"Have you been fucking my sister?"

"I won't lie to you. We've been seeing each other."

"So it's true, you have been fucking her!"

"You have to understand. No one could love Laura as much as I do."

"Oh, well, that's different then. *If you love her, I don't mind you fuckin' her*!" His palpable rage sent a chill down Norm's spine. But then Dave sighed and said, "Alright. If she has to go out with somebody, I'm glad it's you. Put it there…"

When they shook hands, Dave took a fierce grip and yanked him face first into the hydro pole! Norm bounced, tripped over his own feet, fell to the ground and rolled onto his stomach. Dave dropped a knee upon his back, latched onto his hair, and bashed his face into the frozen gravel! After a barrage of blows, Norm passed out.

Dave backed up the car but went too far, covering Norm's body from his hips down. Dave popped the trunk and tugged on Norm's coat…but couldn't budge him—the back tire was parked on his right foot! "DAMN IT!" Dave snapped. A porch light suddenly shined across the alley. Dave drove the Cutlass forward, then dumped his friend into the trunk and slammed the door shut. He floored it taking off but Norm started banging something in the trunk. Dave slammed on the brakes. *I better shut him up!*

He turned the engine off, snatched the keys out of the ignition and lunged to the rear of the car. When he opened the trunk, Norm jabbed him in the eye with a tire iron! "SON-OF-A-BITCH!" Dave yelled. Free flowing rage nullified the pain of his grisly eye injury. Dave wrestled the tire iron from him and raised it, intending to crack his skull—but Norm reached up and slammed the door shut! Dave smashed the trunk with the tire iron till it occurred to him to reuse the key…but it no longer fit into the hole because he'd bashed it out of shape!

"You're gonna wish I finished you off here!" Dave said. He planned to drive upon a frozen patch of Lake Ontario, then let the car coast into the water, where the Wolfe Island ferry maintained an open channel. He'd just resettled in the driver's seat when red lights flashed and sirens blasted behind him. He started the car, pressed the gas pedal to the floor, *and then*, with the engine roaring, rammed the shifter into 'Drive.' The Oldsmobile buckled as the transmission clanged and clanked into pieces!

Laura had just slipped into her silky, pink nightgown when she heard the sirens. She ran to her window and saw red lights flashing against the leafless trees. With her heart racing, she pulled on her housecoat, flew down the stairs, stepped into her snow boots, then bolted outside.

Approaching the police barrier, she saw Norm on a stretcher—his face looked like raw hamburger! "NORM!" she cried out. A police sergeant held her back. "Will he be okay?" she asked.

"His pulse was strong when we arrived on the scene. It's up to the paramedics now. I'm sergeant McCormick. What's your name and how do you know the victim?"

"I'm Laura Needler. He's my boyfriend, Norm Pattison."

She saw the silhouette of her brother's head in the backseat of a cruiser. She dashed past McCormick, opened the door, then jabbed punches at Dave. He sat there laughing, with his hands cuffed behind his back. When she landed a blow to his swollen-shut eye, he laughed even harder!

The sergeant pulled Laura away from the car and slammed the door shut. "Hold on now, missy! There's been enough violence here for one night, don't you think?" Two young officers ran over. "Get him out of here!" McCormick ordered. The cruiser tore off, as did the ambulance.

McCormick draped his jacket over Laura's housecoat, then asked rudimentary questions. She pointed to her house, then explained that the "lunatic" in the back of the cruiser was her stepbrother. He offered to drive Laura to the hospital after she dressed, but she insisted they follow the ambulance right away.

As McCormick clipped along in his cruiser, he said to Laura, "When you're feeling better, I'd like to ask a few more questions."

"There's no need to wait. I can tell you exactly what happened—my stepbrother is a maniac—he tried to kill my boyfriend!" For the rest of the drive, Laura divulged all the pertinent details, including the time Dave tried to rape her.

***

Laura sat in the waiting room with her head buried in her hands. She had gone through an awkward conversation with Norm's parents, standing before them in her pink housecoat, apologizing for her brother's insanity, telling them how much she loved their son. After Laura pleaded for forgiveness, Mrs. Pattison simply said, "STAY AWAY!"

At 3:47 a.m, a doctor told the Pattisons that Norm was in stable condition. When they went to see him, Laura tried to tag along, but was told by Norm's father to "*Back off!*" She collapsed into her chair and cried. A nurse stepped into the waiting area and said, "Excuse me, are you Laura Needler?"

Laura stemmed her flow of tears and nodded.

"We have an urgent call for you."

Laura followed the nurse to the front desk, then picked up the receiver, "Hello?"

"He's alive?"

She nearly choked on her own pounding heartbeat. "What do you care?"

"Laura, I'm sorry! Don't know what got into me. It's like you said, the thing that happened in Mexico had a weird affect on us. How's he doing?"

"He's going to make it—no thanks to you!"

"You didn't tell the cops anything, did you?"

"As a matter of fact, I told them everything!"

"Dad got me an expensive lawyer. If you screwed things up for me—"

"You screwed things up for yourself—I hope you rot in prison!"

"Just because I'm behind bars, doesn't mean I can't get at you! How do you think I was able to call from jail this time of day? I'm like a *god* in here!"

"More like the Devil—I never want to speak to you ever again!"

"Do you really think Norm will have anything to do with you, now?"

"Our relationship is stronger than you know. He loves me."

"We'll see how long that lasts once he finds out I've fucked you!"

Laura slammed down the receiver. Despondent, she staggered out of the hospital and would have wandered aimlessly in her nightgown and housecoat, if it hadn't been for Harrietta, who'd come to pick her up in a black Mercedes.

Chapter Thirteen

The Perth Bay Pikes sat in the change room, about to face the Frontenac Falcons for the final game of the regular season. As coach O'Reilly delved into a zealous pep talk, his spittle flew through the air and landed upon Miles's bobbing knee. A far cry from his former role as bench warmer, Miles was now his team's *sixth man*, the first player O'Reilly subbed into a game. His promotion came with a price: wicked pre-game anxiety!

"We're one win from clinching first place," O'Reilly concluded. "GET OUT THERE AND SHOW 'EM WHO'S NUMBER ONE IN THIS TOWN!"

The Pikes charged out of the change room and into a packed gym. O'Reilly warmed up his team, then let them shoot. Miles nailed seven of eleven jump shots. A buzzer sounded and the Pikes huddled. The coach talked about "grace under fire." In unison, each player raised a hand from the center of the huddle while chanting "GOOOO PIKES!" Miles sat on the bench while the Pikes and Falcons positioned themselves around center court. A ref tossed a jump ball and the game was underway.

Both teams played fast-break basketball. The lead changed hands continuously. Five minutes into the game, Cooke bobbled a pass, which lead to a turnover. The coach yelled down the bench, "Martini—get in for Cookie!"

Miles went to the scorekeeper and subbed into the game. His spry, agile style was well suited for the frantic pace. By the third quarter, he had racked up five points and four assists. The score was tied, 47 all.

Then, to his chagrin, the coach pulled him out of the game. Restless, Miles paced behind the bench. The third quarter ended, then most of the fourth. Miles glanced at the coach and thought, *What to hell are you waiting for? Sub me back in*! With fifty-seven seconds left on the game clock, the Falcons were ahead by a single point. O'Reilly finally hollered, "Martini—get in there for Hornbeak!"

After a whistle, Miles jumped onto the court and sent Hornbeak to the bench. From the sideline near center court, Hank Reddick in-bounded the ball to Miles. The lanky teen dribbled into the offensive zone, pulled up at the top of the key, faked a pass to his center, then rifled the ball to Tate Cooke, near the baseline.

Tate fired a ten foot jump shot. The ball rolled around the rim, then lipped out. Four Pikes crashed the backboard for a rebound; Miles was the only teammate to stay back. The Falcon's center latched onto the ball, then fired an outlet pass to his guard.

Miles ran backwards, in the middle of a two-on-one. When he reached the key, he flashed his hands in the dribbler's face, as if committing to him fully; but Miles was faking, already peeled away as the pass was hurried across the key. He leapt forward and snatched the ball out of the air!

Meanwhile, Hank Reddick had given up. Since he didn't bother to hustle back, he was left alone in the offensive zone—wide open! Miles heaved an overhand pass to Hank, who turned and lunged into long strides. The ball flew over his left shoulder and landed in his outstretched hands. Uncontested, he scored an easy lay-up!

Pike fans rocked the gymnasium with thunderous cheering and applause! With eighteen seconds left on the clock, the Falcon's coach called a timeout.

Huddled with his teammates, Miles heard his coach say, "Nice play, Martini." But after that, he was so consumed with adrenaline, everything blurred; he didn't hear a word as O'Reilly instructed his team to fall back into a zone defence. A buzzer sounded to end the timeout. The coach reiterated: "Remember fellas—NO FOULS!"

As soon as the ball was in-bounded, Miles chased it from one player to another, until one of the guards took it upon himself to dribble. Miles ran over and waved his hands in front of the kid's face. The referee held his whistle near his lips, ready to call a foul, but Miles never committed one.

"MARTINI!" O'Reilly yelled from the bench, "What to hell are you doing? Fall back into position!"

Miles didn't hear his coach; he was too busy angling off the dribbler, who soon found himself trapped between Miles and the sideline. With the game clock running out, with Miles weaving in front of him like a mad cobra, the Falcon guard lobbed a blind pass, hoping a teammate could salvage a shot. But Hank Reddick reached in front of a Falcon forward and deflected the pass with his fingertips. While the ball bounced into the empty half of the court, the crowd chanted, "THREE, TWO—ONE!" and the buzzer sounded to end the game. Ecstatic fans flooded the court and a girl Miles had never met before hugged his sweaty body!

As the two teams shook hands, the Falcon's coach said to O'Reilly, "That kid who went crazy at the end there, was that your idea, or did he do that on his own? I thought for sure your guys would have fallen back into a zone defence."

When O'Reilly joined his team in the change room, he said, "Alright fellas, great game, except Martini—what was that bone-headed play at the end there? I gave you specific instructions to play the left elbow of the 2-1-2 defence. Next time, don't be such a hero—just do as you're told!"

"Yes sir." Miles wondered when his heart would stop pounding like rapid cannon fire.

***

It was unheard of: Sheila Babcock home alone on a Friday night. Miles had stood her up! All day, she'd been thinking about how she'd glisten his lips by hand feeding him a Cornish hen. She licked the tip of her thumb and index finger and snuffed out a candle.

While Sheila chanted in the dark, Miles mingled at a house party. He quaffed a belt of ice cold beer, then said to Jo, "Can't believe how people are treating me. So I helped my team win a basketball game, was it really that big of a deal? I'm still the same guy I've always been."

"What can I say, Pal? You're like a rock star!"

A cute blond approached Miles and said, "You're that basketball guy, right?" Lingering eye contact, discernable warmth in her smile; even without clairvoyance, Miles could tell she liked him. Jo excused himself.

After Vanessa introduced herself, Miles dispensed with small talk, took her hand and led her downstairs, to a rec room, where the luminosity was limited to the dim glow of a TV screen. Amid several entwined teens, lip-locked and groping, Miles plopped upon a cushiony armchair and pulled Vanessa onto his lap. They started with light kissing; but then Vanessa licked his lower lip, and it lead to intense bouts of *tongue tango.*

Meanwhile, Jo was upstairs playing Twister with his *two girlfriends*, Jill and Delores. When he reached under Jill's hip to place his "left hand on yellow," he slipped onto his elbow. Eliminated from the round, he scooped ice cubes out of a nearby cocktail glass, and slipped them down the front of Delores's blouse! As the ice sent shivers down her spine, she fell against Jill and they both collapsed. Amid deep paroxysms of laughter, they tackled Jo and wrestled with him upon the carpet.

It was all ecstatic fun for the buffooning clairvoyant, until he heard three male teens thinking things like, *That's not right...He's weird...They're freaks!* Truth was, those guys didn't have a single girlfriend, let alone two. Jo stepped up to them and said, "We need players for a piggyback fight. Are you guys in?"

The male teens dropped to their knees and a few surrounding girls, who didn't want to miss out on the fun, climbed upon their shoulders. Bodily pileups and laughter ensued. Jo laughed hardest at his new male companions, for he knew having warm muff pressed against the back of their necks had annihilated their animosity, like sudden world peace!

Back in the basement, Vanessa and Miles rounded second base. She smacked her lips off his and whispered, "Do you want to get out of here?"

They headed upstairs. From beneath a heap of frolicking teens, Jo looked up at his cousin. "Hold on, let me see you out." At the front door, he held out his hand. When Miles shook, he received a little packet, with a condom inside.

"Thanks," Miles said, "you think of everything!"

The jolly clairvoyant bid Vanessa adieu. She flashed him a warm smile, then stepped outside with the lanky basketball hero.

Miles escorted Vanessa to the passenger side of his father's blue Impala, where he opened the door for her. They then drove to a quarry, at the outskirts of Kingston. Moonlight reflected off ice that'd been shovelled for shinny. The young couple picked up where they'd left off in the rec room, with hectic necking and frisking, working each other into fever-pitches. After building a thick curtain of steam upon the windows, they pulled off their jeans and Miles opened the condom packet.

"You're not putting that thing on yet, are you?" she said.

"What do you mean?"

She nudged his mouth dewy south. He was reluctant at first, didn't have a clue what to do down there. But once he tasted her womanly spice, there was no stopping him! He went mad licking, lapping, sucking and kissing, till she gasped a mighty O and had to pry his face off her soaking wet lips, dying of sensitivity!

Confident Vanessa had enjoyed the experience *at least* as much as he did, Miles rolled the condom onto his burgeoning erection, slipped inside her wet warmth and exploded after one…two…three deep thrusts!

She waited until his breathing panted back to normal, then said, "See? That's why I wanted you to go down on me first."

"Why?"

"Never mind; you were amazing!"

He tossed the loaded condom out the window and dressed, *tout suite*.

"What's your hurry?" she said, "Is everything alright?"

"I'm just tired. Was up at six this morning for a practice. I'd like to see you again, though, if that's okay."

"Sure, I'd like that."

Miles defrosted the windows, then drove off. When they reached her house, he kissed her cheek and said, "*Goodnight, now.*" As soon as Vanessa was a couple steps from the Impala, he sped off, headed for rural route #66, then turned down Sheila's long, unkempt driveway. Hoping her mother wouldn't mind him calling near the witching hour, he climbed out of the Impala and jumped onto their porch.

When Sheila answered the door, she wore nothing but a silky red robe. "Where t' hell have you been?" Before he could answer, she slapped his face! She then grabbed a fist full of his coat, yanked him close and kissed him madly! After her lips smacked off him, he stammered, "Sorry I'm so late. My cousin dragged me to a party. As you know, he recently came out of the hospital and I couldn't say no to him."

"Well, you're here now, come on in. Can I get you something to drink?"

"A beer would be nice."

After Sheila brought Miles a bottle of Brador (what a teammate recently quipped as "Bra-door" beer), she sat with him on the sofa. After a swig he said, "There's something I've been meaning to get off my chest: When you caught me in bed with your sister, it wasn't my fault! After smoking from that big pipe in your basement, I passed out in the bedroom and when I awoke, Tammy was in bed with me."

"Don't worry, Miles. Ancient history. I sure do miss her though."

"Why? Where'd she go?"

"Whenever Tammy goes off her meds she has visions and hears voices and ends up in a special hospital."

(So the rumours about Tammy being in an asylum were true, Miles thought, *great—I lost my virginity to a madwoman*!)

"I didn't mean to make you feel uncomfortable, Miles."

"No, it's cool. Everybody has their problems."

Sheila started kissing him but suddenly pulled back. "What's that smell on your face?"

His eyes bulged as he realized she was referring to the scent of Vanessa's genitalia! He mumbled something about spicy food served at the party and excused himself.

Miles ducked into the bathroom and washed his face. When he returned to Sheila, she opened her robe, placed her hands on his shoulders and nudged his face down her naked body. As the tip of his tongue slipped passed her bellybutton, it occurred to him she likely knew he'd already gone down on another girl that evening, and wanted some of that action for herself!

Chapter Fourteen

Norm Pattison lay in his hospital bed brooding about the time he helped Dave beat the day lights out of Jo Martini. *Karma's a bitch*! he thought. He envied Stu Seacliff, the third guy who had helped in the beating. Stu's father had been transferred to the States and so the Seacliffs now resided in Philadelphia.

If only it had been me who moved away, Norm thought, then I wouldn't be lying in this constant agony! Mummy-like bandages covered his mangled face. He breathed through his mouth because the cartilage in his nose had been disjointed. Four of his front teeth had been bashed out. Opiates helped but his headache was incessant.

Worse than his physical injuries, Norm couldn't stop shuddering. For the the rest of his life, he'd be looking over his shoulder. He kept picturing how Needler would finish him off: a knife in his back, a baseball bat cracking his skull, a car dragging his naked body down a gravel road!

The phone rang beside his bed. He ignored it. Laura had been calling him morning, noon and night. He used to wonder why Dave was so insanely jealous of his sister; now, he didn't care! With twenty-seven stitches around his eyes, Norm saw her in a different light.

A nurse entered his room and passed him an envelop with Laura's handwriting on the front. A sudden terrifying thought stopped him from dropping it into a waste basket: *What if she's trying to warn me about her brother? What if Dave was released on bail—on his way to the hospital this very moment!* Norm tore open the envelop and read:

Dearest Norm,

Please stop avoiding me because of my brother's insanity! You must believe my love for you is stronger than his hate. And consider this: Not only was Dave caught red handed, but also, he's nineteen years old, so he'll be tried as an adult. This means there's not an overpriced lawyer in the world who can prevent him from doing serious time!

Obviously, you've been through a lot. But I can't go on suffering like this alone. Please call me right away. I miss you with all my heart!

Yours in eternal love,

Laura

Norm's facial bandages absorbed a stream of tears. He picked up the phone and called her.

***

Meanwhile, Dave paced a couple steps to and fro, in his 3X5 meter cell. A black patch covered his eye, maimed by Norm during their brawl. At least she hasn't visited him yet, he thought, relieved by what a couple of spying nurses had told him. *Damn it! How am I gonna get out of this bloody mess*? He punched the cement wall, wrapped his bleeding knuckles with toilet paper, then resumed his quick, two-step pacing.

***

Laura burst into Norm's room and released heavy tears of relief while embracing him.

"You were right," Norm said, "Our love has to be stronger than his hate."

She sat on the edge of his bed. Besides her calf-skin coat, Norm was looking at a version of her he'd never seen before. Her hair was tangled, her eyes were red and puffy. Nevertheless, she was still the most beautiful girl he'd ever seen.

"Please Norm, promise you'll never, ever shut me out like that again!"

"I promise."

She eased her head onto his chest and they consoled each other with tender, resuscitating caresses. The phone rang and Norm picked up the receiver, "Hello?"

"Do you really think I can't get to you just because I'm locked up?"

Norm started to shake. "You have some nerve calling me here!"

Laura's eyes shifted fitfully. "Don't listen to him—hang up!"

"She's with you right now, isn't she?" Dave said.

"What? No!"

"Norm, Norm, Norm—YOU'RE SUCH A MORON! There's no point in lying—I have eyes everywhere! I know for a fact she's with you this very second."

"What do you want?"

"Guess I'll have to spell it out for you. I have plenty of contacts in Kingston. If you don't break it off with Laura, I'm gonna start with your parents. It might be a fire, or a car accident—or a baseball bat while they sleep!" (Norm remembered Dave used similar threats after beating Jo Martini.) "You still there Norm? You must be cuz I can hear your choppy, wimp-ass breathing. After your parents die, I'll send someone for **you**! And the beauty of it is, when you're in a ditch somewhere, laying in a pool of your own blood, I'll have an airtight alibi, cuz I'll be locked up!"

"Listen, you sick son of a bitch, threaten me all you want. Laura and I are in love—we're meant to be together!"

"Really? Why do you think that? Because you fucked her? Well, *welcome to the club*! Haven't you ever wondered why I've always been so protective of her? She's not my real sister, moron! Understand? Comprende?"

"What?" Norm said choking on a single syllable. Though Laura had warned him about this "grotesque lie," the conviction in Dave's voice rattled him.

"Don't listen to him," Laura said, "Hang up!"

"That's right ol' buddy," Dave continued, "She's mine—right down to the birthmark on her ass, the one shaped like Texas!"

Norm cringed. It was all the proof he needed. "Alright Needler, you win. Nothing will happen to my parents, right?"

"Keep away from Laura and I'll forget I ever knew you."

Norm slammed down the receiver and said to Laura, "GET OUT!"

She latched onto him and begged for forgiveness. He pressed a button beside his bed. When a nurse stepped into the room, he said, "GET HER OUT OF HERE!"

The nurse called security. Moments later, two burly men pried Laura off Norm. When they dragged her into an elevator, she went limp. When they released her in the front foyer, she slumped through automatic doors. The cold night air didn't affect her—she was already numb inside. At a bus stop, she sat upon a bench and laid her head to the side.

***

Laura awoke in her own bed as a family physician took her pulse. "How are you feeling, dear?"

She rolled onto her side, turning her back on him. "Well," the doctor said to Mrs. Needler, "she doesn't have frostbite. She's not suffering from hypothermia. Physically, she's fine; but emotionally?"

"Laura," Harrietta said, "I realize you've been through a lot, but I have some huge news."

Oh my God, Laura thought, *Norm is dead*! She sat up. "What is it mother?"

"Your stepfather has taken off with Eva, our Yugoslavian maid. It's why I didn't meet you at the hospital. I've been dealing with a crisis of my own."

After a sigh of relief, Laura laughed hysterically. The doctor pricked a needle into her arm and her eyes turned glassy. "I'm sorry for your sake, mom. But don't you see? The monster maker is gone; good riddance to him!" She yawned uncontrollably as the tranquilizer knocked her out.

The doctor wrote on his prescription pad and tore off the top sheet. "Here," he said to the harried mother, "this is the best psychiatrist in town. She's going to need professional help."

Harrietta crumpled the paper into a ball and tossed it into a waste basket. "She doesn't need a psychiatrist. In my experience, a little trauma makes one stronger. You see doctor, we're survivors."

Chapter Fifteen

While Laura's mood turned icy blue in the cold bleak winter, Norm's disposition warmed considerably. His uncle Jared had phoned him from Jamaica: "Come work for me mon—*you be jammin'*." As soon as Norm was fit to travel, he'd fly south and work for his uncle's company, sailing tourists around the turquoise waters of the Caribbean sea.

Not only had Laura lost her lover forever, but also, she'd been abandoned by her friends, every one of them repulsed by her scandalous family. Amid the sudden and thorough alienation, Laura tried to forget about her maniacal brother. For the most part, she managed to shun him from her thoughts. But when she was alone in the dark, visions of Dave haunted her. She'd see him in the alleyway, smashing Norm's face to pulp; she'd see her brother's foreskin retract and sense it between her legs like the muted screams of Medusa.

Because the images only terrified her in the dark, Laura pulled the blankets off her bed and slept on the floor, directly beneath her chandelier, its dimmer switch cranked to full luminosity. It started to make perfect sense to her: light was her solitary ally against the nightmarish memories of her stepbrother.

The next day, she stared at her own personal infernos in the fireplace. That evening, she stared at a light bulb in her vanity table. Harrietta barged into her room and said, "What to heck are you doing?"

When Laura looked towards the door, her pupils were so constricted, they blotted her field of vision. "Ever heard of knocking?"

"Dinner's ready."

"Could you ask Martha to light candles?"

Laura let her eyes adjust to ambient light, then joined her mother in the dining room. Harrietta said, "Don't get upset, but I need you to read this letter from your brother."

Laura convulsed. "ARE YOU OUT OF YOUR MIND?"

Harrietta set an envelope before her daughter, then said, "If we appear sympathetic towards Dave Jr., it'll seem like we're dealing with a mess the father left behind and the divorce court will see this in a favourable light." (Laura stared unwaveringly at the candlelight.) "Are you listening, missy? Your stepfather has abandoned us. Help me clean the son of a bitch out! Don't forget: when I die, every cent will go to you."

Laura wanted to set a corner of the envelop into the flame of the candle. But Harrietta said, "We're survivors. We shouldn't do anything to louse up our win-fall." Eventually, Laura snatched the envelop off the table and tore it open:

Dear Laura,

To write you I barely feel worthy. But its importent my shrink says. You once said the thing that happened to us in Mexico had a wierd effect on us. You were right about that! If I didn't talk you into meeting those Mexicans, they wouldn't of attacked us. If they didn't attack us, I wouldn't of gotten obsessed with you. If I didn't get obsessed with you, I wouldn't of gotten mad when I found out about you and Norm. So it gos in life that one terrible mistake often laeds to another.

I have hostility issues because of dad my shrink says. Living with him you know what it was like. I acted like him I'm sorry. And now

he's taken off on us. First I loose you, then him. I'm so alone. Don't know what I'll do if you don't write me back.
Love, your brother,
Dave

When Laura finished reading the letter, she went ahead and held it over the candle. Her mother doused the burning paper with a glass of water. "I understand you're stressed but you have to get used to the idea Dave will be in your life for a little while longer. You have to think logically about this. Have you forgotten I work at a law firm? Trust me, Dave will serve the longest sentence possible. After the divorce is settled, you can turn your back on him forever."

Oblivious to her mother's lecture, Laura surveyed the various sources of luminosity. The candlelight, the chandelier and—the dim rays of the setting sun beaming through the patio window. *The sun.* OF COURSE, THE SUN! She sang in her head, *Oh Mr. Sun, Sun / Mr. Golden Sun / Please shine down on me.*

"By the way," Harrietta said, "will you ever wash your hair again? How about getting dressed every once in a while? You have to pull yourself together!"

After dinner, Laura went to the family library and dug out everything she could find on the sun. As she pored over texts, she was inspired by Galileo and Newton since both scientists observed the sun with their naked eyes. When she read that ancient Chinese emperors commissioned citizens to stare at sunspots, her life's ambition became clear as day.

The following morning, Laura bundled up in ski wear, then went outdoors and pulled out a lawn chair from the back shed. Seated facing south, she crossed her feet upon a crusty layer of snow, lowered tinted goggles over her eyes and glanced repeatedly at the sun. By dusk she felt satiated by bright light, her anxiety effectively whitewashed for the day.

After a week of observation, she was able to stare at the sun without the goggles. Since retinas don't have pain receptors, she barely felt anything as solar radiation cooked her eyeballs. Meanwhile, her sight away from intense light developed black voids, as if sunspots were permanent fixtures in her field of vision. This new impairment led to a sudden accumulation of bruises, caused by her new tendency to bump into things.

One morning during breakfast, Harrietta handed her daughter another letter. All Laura could see was a series of blurred lines. While she pretended to read, the sun beckoned her like a siren. She rushed to pour milk on her cereal but missed the bowl!

"*Jesus-H-Christ, Laura*—WAKE UP!" her mother scolded.

The milk ran off the table and soaked the lap of Laura's pyjamas. "May I be excused?"

"It's time you went back to school—before your brain turns to mush! You can have the rest of the week off, but then—"

"Mother! May I please be excused?"

"Alright, enjoy the rest of your *holiday*. But before you go, tell me, have you responded to your brother's first letter?"

Laura used a serviette to soak milk out of her pyjama bottoms.

"Stop ignoring me!" Harrietta said.

"Whatever, mother. I'll do it later." Laura made her way to the closet, bundled up in ski wear, then assumed her position outdoors upon the lawn chair. She counted two sunspots that morning, each tiny dot more precious to her than the Hope Diamond.

Later that day, a servant went to the shed for sidewalk salt. The site of Laura's solar trance horrified him! He ran inside and called her mother, who dropped everything at work and sped home. She found Laura in a daze while gazing at a single, solitary star. "My God, you're mutilating your eyes—come inside this minute!"

Laura snapped out of her solar trance and looked towards Harrietta but could only see blotchy darkness. "Don't be mad at me, okay? I'll send a letter to Dave as soon as the sun sets."

Harrietta felt too consumed by her divorce to deal with her disturbed daughter, who was now functionally blind. She had Laura committed to the O.H (Ontario Hospital), Kingston's limestone asylum. A substantial, under-the-table fee, paid to the head administrator, bought Laura extra protection from fellow patients.

***

Laura's first couple weeks at the O.H went by surprisingly well. Despite repugnant odors that permeated her ward, despite piercing screams that occasionally awoke her in the night, she began to feel at ease with herself. Perhaps the real nuthouse was the mansion she'd been living in! Her rapid progress had been facilitated by an elderly psychologist named Dr. May, an existentialist who had the comfy aura of a six-foot teddy bear.

After several daily sessions of intense talk therapy, he said to Laura, "Let me summarize what we've uncovered so far: You hate your brother, which is perfectly understandable after everything he's done to you. Although, I hope you come to realize one day, everyone, from Gandhi to Hitler, is the way they are because of how they experience the world. You attempted to obliterate Dave from your thoughts by staring at bright light, which escalated to *heliomania,* an excessive love of the sun. Now, here's the sixty million dollar question: Why not choose to exist elsewhere?"

"You mean move away from Kingston, like my ex-boyfriend did?"

"Not necessarily. I was referring to your ability to exist elsewhere in your thoughts."

"Are you saying the pain I feel is my fault because I 'choose' to think of Dave?"

"Well, yes and no. Dave's a psychopath who could leave deep, emotional scars on anyone. But he's locked up now, out of your life in the physical sense. Doesn't this mean you're free to direct your thoughts away from him?"

"It can't be that simple!"

"Does it have to be that complicated?"

"What if I can never get him out of my head?"

"But you've already done it to a degree, with your fixation on bright light. Letting him go, without extreme, self-defeating measures, only seems impossible because he has terrified you to such an extent, you've developed a massive, emotional investment in him. Let me ask you this: why do people watch horror movies?"

"Something to do with an emotional investment?"

"Precisely! Being scared gives people a rush, a chemical reaction in their brains, like an addictive drug that distracts them from their problems."

"So thinking about Dave is like being addicted to a drug, a habit I must *kick* to be happy again?"

"Precisely! You don't want to waste the bulk of your existence thinking about Dave. Where else might you direct your mental energy?"

"I'm not sure."

"Let's start with something fundamental." He passed her a set of headphones. "Try to distinguish the individual instruments and tie them in with the lyrics. The idea is to focus on the music with the intensity you previously devoted to the sun."

She set the headphones over her ears and Dr. May played a song by the band Steely Dan. Intrigued, Laura concentrated on the music. Before long, she was tapping her fingers and toes. Near the end of the song, a tear rolled down her cheek.

The doctor removed the headphones. "What is it Laura? Why are you crying?"

"I get it, Dr. May. Focusing on music is an example of choosing to direct my thoughts away from my brother, thereby existing elsewhere in my mind. I also understand why you wanted me to listen to those particular lyrics: *Get back Jack, do it again / Wheels turnin' round and around.* I've probably heard that song a hundred times and never knew what it meant. 'Do it Again' is about the doom of addiction, as depicted by gamblers who compound their troubles with other bad habits, such as crime and self-defeating relationships. Meanwhile, guitars, chimes, bongos, maracas and an organ, create a hypnotic rhythm, like how obsessions hold us spellbound.

"It occurs to me my family has been obsessed with its superior status. I was always so worried about having the best, most expensive clothes, I missed out on more meaningful experiences. And that was going on long before the trouble started with my brother." She paused to reflect. "How could a single song lead me to so many insights?"

"Clearly, you were overdue for a breakthrough, likely knew something was awry for many years, but it took a trauma for you to gain a fresh perspective. You see Laura, when emotional barriers are broken, enlightenment often flows in a stream of consciousness. It reminds me of a Zen metaphor. Imagine you're in a fast flowing river, holding on to an overhanging branch. Overcome by exhaustion, you let go and the current carries you away. This is analogous to how a healthy release of emotion can prompt thoughts to flow."

"So, releasing the branch is like letting go of my emotional ties to Dave. This frees the flow of my thoughts, to find healthier places to be in my own head. I can channel this flow anywhere I choose: the scent of a rose, the taste of a fresh strawberry, the lyrics of a great song—the possibilities are endless! How can I ever thank you doctor?"

"Believe me, seeing you come alive like this is all the thanks I need. Great work Laura! Let me walk you to your braille class."

During her class, Laura found unexpected pleasure in sliding her fingers over the smooth, metal nodes. Like her sense of hearing, her sense of touch was now flourishing.

That evening after dinner, the raven haired beauty listened to the rhythms of a ping-pong ball bouncing to and fro. Earlier that day, a patient had smashed a chair into a window, cracking the safety glass. Starved for a new sensation, Laura felt her way along the wall, to where a burly maintenance man was packing up his tools. Dumbfounded by her beauty, he watched her feel around the window cell, where she found a leftover wad of glazing putty. Sensing his eyes on her, she asked if she could keep it. He stammered, "I really shouldn't...aw, what t' heck, go ahead."

Later, alone in her room, Laura squeezed the putty with the delight of a child who'd just discovered Play-doh. She removed her shoes and socks, then squished the pliable substance between her toes. There was a knock at her door and a soft, feminine voice said, "I don't mean to intrude but I love cats."

"I don't understand," Laura said, "Is there a cat in here?"

"No, but I'm curious by nature, like cats. Wondered what you took from the workman."

"Come on in. I'll show you."

The young woman sat beside Laura on the bed. "So that's what you took. May I have some?" Laura gave her half the putty. The stranger squeezed it between her fingers. "Smooth, cool and squishy. I like the feel of it."

"I like it too. Guess we should introduce ourselves."

"Everyone knows who you are, Laura. I'm Tammy Babcock."

"Pleased to meet you Tammy."

"So how did the *Cleopatra of Kingston* end up in a place like this?"

After Laura explained her blinding affair with the sun, her new acquaintance said, "This must be a case of opposites attracting. Whereas you love the sun and light of day, I worship the moon and darkness of night."

"You worship the moon?"

"Among other things. It's part of my heritage. My aunt's a Wiccan priestess."

"So you're a witch?"

"It's why I'm in this bin. When I'm not doped out on meds, I have visions."

"I suppose one person's vision is another's idea of madness."

"Exactly! What we practice is no more crazy than what's found in other religions. For instance, is it rational to obsess over a man with nails through his hands and feet, pretend to drink his blood and eat his flesh? Millions act as if it's perfectly sane! Yet, when I anointed myself with snake oil, they locked me up."

"That's why you're here, because you covered yourself with snake oil and had a vision?"

"Yeah, but I did it on a Friday night. The mall was packed. Children were lined up to see Santa Claus."

Laura stifled her laugh…till they both cracked up, uproariously! After the laughter, Tammy said, "You have beautiful hair. Mind if I brush it?"

Laura reached for her night table, found her brush and passed it to Tammy, who knelt behind her on the bed. "Can I tell you something that might sound a little crazy?"

"We're in the right place for that!" Laura said.

"I faked taking my meds today and had a vision about us meeting this evening."

"Intriguing. What happens next?"

"You're seeking new sensations, right?"

"Whoa—how'd you know?"

"Look how you took to the putty! Also, I sensed it in my vision. Here's my proposition: In exchange for a lock of you hair, I promise you a full bodied sensation that'll blow your mind and rock your world—an experience, of which you've never imagined in your wildest dreams!"

"A little hair seems like a small price to pay. How will you cut it?"

"I have a razor in my shoe."

"How'd you get a razor in a place like this?"

"Whereas you hold men spellbound with your beauty, I simply place them under spells." Tammy pulled the razor out of her shoe and sawed off a strand of Laura's thick black, hair. "Now for my end of the bargain. Have you ever been anointed?"

"Other than things like skin cream and suntan lotion, can't say I have."

"This'll definitely be different than that! Take off your clothes and stand naked before me." Tammy pulled a bottle of clear oil from her waistband. "I should warn you, Laura. The first time can be intense. Just hold on and ride the waves of ecstasy."

***

The next morning, Laura met Tammy at the Jacuzzi, part of their relaxation therapy. The raven haired beauty, minus a lock of hair, slid next to her new friend in the bubbly hot water. "Hope your ointment doesn't wash off easily. My skin still tingles, from head to toe—never slept a wink all night! What's in that stuff anyway, snake oil?"

"Laura, you're an outsider; if I told you, you'd either have to join us, or I'd have to silence you—*permanently*!"

"Okay…sorry, didn't mean to offend you."

"It's alright. You're not versed in the ways of Wicca, though you could be."

"It's Friday, are you watching the movie tonight?"

"No, I have a weekend pass. Goin' home this afternoon."

The soothing jets lulled the girls into a deep state of calm, the weight of the world reduced to the swirling molecules of 104 degree water. Eventually, a staff member, a black grandmotherly attendant, insisted they get out of the tub. The two friends slipped out of the bubbly hot water and showered together.

Laura inhaled one last whiff of the ointment before her Wiccan friend washed it off her back, neck and shoulders. When they came out of the shower, their naked bodies were covered in shivers. The attendant handed them towels. Laura dried off, then slipped into a cozy cotton sweater, its soft warmth nestled against her cold, hard nipples. She stepped into her panties, then pulled on a pair of grey sweatpants. "You know Tammy, I never noticed it before, but these casual clothes are so comfortable."

"Tammy's not here," the black lady said, "she scooped up her clothes and hightailed it down the hall."

***

That afternoon in Dr. May's office, Laura discussed her latest revelation: "…When I slipped into a sweater and sweatpants, my former wardrobe became an enigma to me. Clearly, I'd been chafing my body with tight, restrictive clothes. When I wore designer jeans, for instance, they were so tight, I used to lie back on my bed and slide the end of a coat hanger into the zipper tab, just to do them up! I also own a slew of shoes that were murder on my feet, knees and back. It just wasn't natural to walk around with my heels jammed into my calves. One of the first things I'll do when I go home is throw away most of the clothes."

"I think you're onto something, Laura. Us men often suffer the same affliction. Restrictive, buttoned up shirts, ties like nooses, dress shoes not fit to walk around the block in. Meanwhile, a lack of activity leads to obesity, heart disease and diabetes. If loose, athletic clothing was the everyday norm, people would be more inclined to walk, take the stairs, *to move*! No doubt this would improve the overall health of Canadians."

He paused to reflect, then added, "I just realized something paradoxical: not only would athletic clothing enable people to be more physically fit; but also, it'd help them to relax, mentally. For over thirty years, I've been trying to help disturbed individuals calm down and feel at ease with themselves; the whole while, I've been wearing restrictive suits and shirts with starched collars. What kind of example have I been setting? As I speak, I'm pulling off my tie and loosening my collar. I feel like burning all my ties, the way feminists burned their bras in the 60s!"

"Right on, Dr. May!"

"Well, that's it Laura: When you start providing profound insights for the therapist, it's time to leave this place! I'll draw up the paperwork and have you home for dinner. Let me walk you to your exercise class."

He stood, forever tie-less, a patch of grey chest hair protruding from the top of his loosened shirt. Laura rose from her chair. He touched the back of her elbow to guide her out of the office. She turned and latched onto him. Tears fell out her dark glasses. "Sorry Dr. May, this is probably against the rules."

"It's okay Laura, to heck with the rules—a hug is a magical thing!" He allowed himself to hold her for several precious seconds.

"I was dying before I met you," she said, "Thanks for everything."

"You did the work! You're an extraordinary young woman. I'll call your mother and have you released before dinner."

***

Harrietta rushed through the front corridor and held Laura with the urgency of a non-swimmer grasping onto a life preserver in the middle of a stormy sea.

"Mom! I'm happy to see you too, but I need to breathe!"

Harrietta looked her over. The black sunglasses and white cane would take some getting used to. *But sweatpants*? "Let's get you home and into some decent clothes."

"Mother—these are the most decent clothes in the world! When I get home, I'll throw away most of my wardrobe!"

"Whatever you say, dear." (A male patient, wearing a blue chequered shirt with frayed, cut-off sleeves, growled at the Needler women while flexing his sinewy biceps.) "Come on Laura, let's get you out of here."

While they cruised down the highway in Harrietta's black Mercedes, Laura said, "What was that all about back at the hospital?"

"Whatever do you mean, dear?"

"I thought you were going to crack my spine, you held me so tight!"

"Laura, when you left, I was devastated! I realize I haven't been the greatest mother but there were extenuating circumstances. An explanation is long overdue."

"It wasn't all your fault, mom. I learned in therapy our family missed out on meaningful experiences because of our obsession with social status."

"You're probably right...I've never heard you talk like that before. Still, there are some things I need to explain. For instance, Ted Dunn isn't your biological father."

"*Pardon me*?"

"I should've told you long ago but never had the courage. What have I ever told you about my childhood?"

"Not much. You grew up in a trailer park, right?"

"Yes, your grandmother and I lived at the Weller Ave Trailer Park, under assumed names to escape my abusive father. It was a 'fire into the frying pan' situation as those thinly fabricated walls festered with all sorts of undesirables. I'll spare you the gory details; but if you knew what I went through, perhaps you'd forgive me for—" Tears streamed down her cheeks. She pulled over and stopped upon the gravel shoulder. "Laura, I'm so sorry for being such a cold, distant mother."

Laura embraced her. "Obviously, you had a difficult childhood. No wonder you had trouble getting close to anyone, even me."

"Thanks for your understanding, dear." Harrietta dried her eyes with a silky handkerchief. "When I was sixteen, I went out with a boy who'd definitely have the means to free me from the park. His name was Doug McLean. Besides being the proverbial tall, dark and handsome, he was the son of a neurosurgeon. We went to different high schools: he was in grade thirteen at Regi; I was in grade eleven at Q.E. We met when I snuck into a dance at his school.

"From that first night in the backseat of his Trans Am, we shared a raw, animal magnetism—couldn't keep our hands off each other, a passion so torrid, natural and beautiful, we fell madly in love. He often skipped hockey practice to steal away with me. One night he said, 'If I had to choose between scoring the Stanley Cup winning goal, or making love with you, I'd choose you *every time*!'"

"Aw," Laura said, "Sounds romantic. So my real father's name is Doug McLean. What ever happened to him?"

"Well, I thought I had it made. When I told Doug I was pregnant, he proposed to me on the spot. He'd already been accepted at Queen's, destined to be a doctor like his father. But then one night, after driving me home from a prenatal class, he was killed in a terrible car crash. At his wake, his parents made it clear they weren't about to take in any trailer trash.

"That's when I latched onto a surrogate father for you. You might remember, Ted worked at a gas station near Weller Ave. He used to ogle me when I stood at the bus stop in front of his shop. One afternoon, he offered to give me a lift and I let him drive me to a doctor's appointment. He didn't care I was carrying another man's child—he married me when I was seven months pregnant! After you were born, I decided it'd be easier to let you believe Ted was your real father. To his credit, he loved you like you were his own flesh and blood."

"So why'd you leave him?"

"Ted made a decent living as a mechanic, but I had my sights set much higher. After all, I'd almost married a doctor. I'd just been hired as a legal secretary when Dave Sr. retained Berger & Kerr. The lawsuits involved safety violations at his plant. He flirted with me relentlessly and I couldn't resist moving up to the opulent lifestyle I swore I'd live, back when I was poor in the trailer park."

"You were determined to separate yourself as far as possible from the hardship of your youth. Guess it made you kinda callous and emotionally unavailable."

"That's about to change! When you were away, I realized how much I'd been taking motherhood for granted." Harrietta kissed her cheek, then pulled the Mercedes back onto the road, her tires spitting gravel before gripping the pavement.

***

That night, Harrietta agreed to try Dr. May's technique of distinguishing instruments within a song. Laura insisted her mother wear sweatpants. Harrietta was secretly appalled but determined to appease her daughter. She cuddled an arm around Laura as they sat on a sofa in the family room.

As they listened to the jazz station, J.Z FM, a clarinet played to the rhythm of fluttering butterflies. A sax scattered notes like bullfrogs hopping lily pads. A pianist whisked across a keyboard like a sudden breeze rippling the surface of a calm lake. The snazzy nuances of jazz enthralled the mother and daughter for over an hour.

On a commercial break, Harrietta said, "For years now, we've owned the most expensive stereo equipment on the market; yet, I never appreciated how wonderful it sounded. Not until now. And I can't believe I'm about to say this, but these sweatpants are extremely comfortable! Can't remember the last time I've felt this relaxed."

Laura smiled so broadly, her sunglasses high-jumped the bridge of her nose. She laid her head upon her mother's lap and Harrietta stroked her long black hair. "You know Laura, I think your hair is softer now, even more beautiful since you stopped using a hair dryer."

"There's a real knack to fixing my hair this way but I prefer soft to torched."

Harrietta laughed. "You used to spend a half hour a day blow drying your hair. Clearly, you're not the same girl you used to be."

Chapter Sixteen

Sheila Babcock didn't have an athletic bone in her curvaceous body, yet maintained a "B" average in phys ed. It was Friday, her favourite day to attend school, and so she made an appearance in her grade twelve archery class, taught by Mr. O'Reilly (or "Mr. O" as he was affectionately called by female students). Sheila, wearing nothing but a black bodysuit and runners, released the taut string of her bow and the arrow crashed into a cement block, about six feet high and left of the target. O'Reilly grimaced then grinned. "Having trouble Sheila? Let me help you."

He draped himself against her backside, inhaled her heady, Opium perfume…and helped steady the bow. "Left arm straight, good…now, when you exhale, release it smoothly…great shot Sheila!" At least she caught a piece of the target, about a foot low and left of the bull's eye. Meanwhile, other students could have been playing chicken, or acting out Robin Hood fantasies and O'Reilly would have been oblivious!

Because Sheila never recoiled from him, but instead, led him on to a certain extent, Mr. O fantasized about her with reckless abandon. Secretly, he would have given up his family, his job, his position in the community, all to run away with the bodacious Ms. Babcock—he would have done so with a devilish gleam in his eyes and hellfire spouting from his proud cock! If only she weren't so weird and erratic he would have risked everything to pursue her.

At the end of gym class, students secured the archery equipment in a storage room; they were then dismissed. Mr. O'Reilly was about to duck into his office when he saw Miles meet Sheila down the hallway. As she stood on her toes to neck with him, her bodysuit wedged into the crevice of her buttocks. Exasperated, O'Reilly locked himself in his office, lit a cigarette and cursed Miles for having what no gym teacher in his right mind could ever have.

When he came out of his office several minutes later, Miles and Sheila were *still* down the hall sucking face! "Hey you two, get to class!" Under his breath he added, "*Or do I have to toss a bucket of cold water on ya?*"

Sheila flashed a coquettish smile at Mr. O, then scurried into the change room. Miles turned beet red. Late for chemistry class, he bolted down the hallway, burst through a pair of swinging doors and bumped into Vanessa, the chick he'd met last Friday at the party. She stared at the bulge in his pants. "*Pretty classy walking around like that*! Let me guess: you were just with that bitch, Sheila Babcock?"

Speechless, he covered his boner with both hands, interlocking his fingers, as if standing politely at a formal occasion. Vanessa slapped his face—"So the rumours are true! You went to see Sheila right after we did it in the car. That's why you were in such a hurry to leave me. *Hope she gave you V.D*!" She broke into tears and stormed off.

Miles held his cheek where she had slapped him. He'd never felt so ambivalent in all his life. On the one hand, he felt like scum; on the other hand, he'd had sex with two gorgeous gals the same night and it bolstered his male ego like a shot of bovine testosterone!

At home that evening, Miles felt feverish and weak. He wondered if Vanessa's curse had come true. Had Sheila given him V.D? *I can't be sick now*, he thought, *not when the championship game is in six days*! Anton looked into his son's room. "Your mother said you missed dinner. Are you okay Pal?"

Miles described his symptoms with such angst, Anton drove him to the hospital. After sitting in the waiting room for three hours, a nurse escorted Miles to an examination room. She took his temperature, then said a doctor would see him shortly. Before long, a Pakistani intern greeted him and inspected his chart.

"You're a doctor," Miles said, "I should be able to tell you anything, right?"

"Of course, what is it?"

"I've been seeing this girl who's kinda on the wild side and…how do I say it…I might have picked something up from her."

"You mean like mononucleosis?" (Apparently, the young doctor couldn't fathom Miles had been sexually active.)

"Mononucle what?"

"It's also know as mono or the kissing disease."

"That could be it! If so, how long until I can play basketball again?"

"About four weeks."

"*FOUR WEEKS*? But the championship game is on Saturday!"

"Let's not jump to any conclusions. There's a nasty flu going around." The young doctor performed an examination and had the nurse collect a tube of blood.

Miles went home and slept for fourteen hours. Shortly thereafter, a nurse phoned to assure him he had nothing but the flu.

***

The lanky teen was ready to run again in three days. When he rejoined his team, however, his coach centered him out: "What happened, Martini? You missed two practices!"

"I called and told you sir, I had the flu."

"Pish! I played some of the best basketball of my life when I had the flu."

***

Game day. The Perth Bay Pikes versus the Sydenham Golden Eagles. A crew from Kingston's cable network had set up to broadcast the game. Like everyone else in the stands, Jo and his two girlfriends watched the warm-ups with great anticipation. Miles looked sharp, swishing seven of nine jump shots. Sheila Babcock was nowhere to be found.

The ref blew his whistle and the two teams retreated to their respective benches. The Pikes huddled and O'Reilly said, "Alright fellas, this is what we've worked for all season. Remember, Sydenham has a tendency to dog it getting' back on defence—fire outlet passes to Reddick or Hornbeak and we'll dominate on the fast break. And don't forget to box out—show Sydenham some teeth beneath those boards! The headline in Monday's Wig Standard should read, '*Pike Bites Clip Eagles' Wings*!'"

"YES, SIR!" the whole team replied. They each placed a fist into the middle of the huddle, then raised their arms while chanting, "GOOOO PIKES!"

Miles assumed his position on the bench. The referee tossed a jump-ball at center court and the game was under way. Brisk passing, fast breaks, scraps on the floor for loose balls—it was the type of game Miles thrived in. Five minutes passed. Usually, he'd be subbed in by now. But O'Reilly went with Dave Corbett, a portly Pike with a deadly set shot. Miles panicked, *What if the coach doesn't play me*? That won't happen, he assured himself, all my hard work and dedication has to account for something.

By the end of the first half, all his hard work and dedication had accounted for nothing—Miles continued to sit on the bench. Corbett had come out of the game wreaking of sweat and Absorbine Junior. The Pikes were down by four points.

Half way through the third quarter, both teams were showing signs of fatigue. O'Reilly made his fifth substitution, putting Cooke back into the game. A voice in Miles's head yelled, *Cooke again? But I'm totally fresh—put ME in!*

O'Reilly was right about Sydenham being slow coming back on defence. With a couple minutes remaining, the Pikes had racked up enough fast break points to lead by five. The refs facilitated the rapid pace of play by calling few fouls. Next thing Miles knew, the crowd was chanting, "5-4-3-2-1!" The buzzer sounded. The Pikes won 57-54.

Miles walked onto the court, *like the rest of the spectators*. He held back his tears while congratulating his teammates. After shaking hands with the Golden Eagles, he lined up with his team to receive the trophy. When an official draped a medal around his neck, he could no longer hold back his tears. Onlookers likely thought he was overjoyed. Then, Bob Payne stepped out of the crowd and sucker punched Miles, splitting his lip!

***

Later that night, the Pikes met at The Ports Pub. Miles wasn't about to sit there with a fat lip and a lump in his throat, while his teammates celebrated their championship. But then he tossed back several belts of rye from his father's bar, grew pugnacious, stole twenty bucks from his mother's purse, and jumped on a bus.

He strutted into the bar and sat at one of the two parallel tables his team had claimed. He gulped his beer as if sitting alone. Half way through his fifth pint he said, “Thanks for benching me, coach—*ya prick*!”

Mr. O’Reilly, who sat behind Miles at the other table, turned to face him. “If you had shown up for practices, you wouldn’t have to worry about it.”

“I had the flu—big friggin’ deal! I busted my ass for you all season!”

“Your teammates can handle their booze, Martini; with a last name like yours, I would have thought—”

“DON’T CHANGE THE SUBJECT—BE A MAN—TELL ME THE REAL REASON YOU BENCHED ME!”

“His big mouth will get you guys kicked out of here,” O’Reilly said to the other players.

“Don’t worry sir,” Hank Reddick said, “We’ll take care of him.”

Hank, Tate and Art grabbed Miles and dragged him out the backdoor. “Thanks for sticking up for me,” Miles said, “Bunch of frickin’ weasels!”

They pushed him to the ground and went back into the bar. Miles staggered to his feet, stretched out upon the hood of an old Pontiac, then passed out. Before long, Jo and his two girlfriends were pulling him off the car. When they poured Miles into the Pinto, he bonked his head on the threshold. The drunken teen said, “That should have hurt, right?”

“You’ll probably feel it in the morning,” Jill said.

He lay across the backseat and rested his head upon Delores’s lap. “How’d you guys find me?”

“We heard after the game the Pikes were meeting at The Ports,” Jo said, “Kind of ironic what happened at the end there, when Bob Payne sucker punched you.”

“No big deal. I understand where he was coming from.”

“Why’d you take off on us after the game?” Jill said.

“I needed to be alone.”

“No wonder you were upset,” Delores said, “What was your coach’s problem? Why didn’t he play you?”

“He was mad because I missed a couple of practices, due to the flu.”

“That’s ridiculous!” Delores said, “You should never workout when you have a fever. Besides, you could’ve spread the flu to your teammates and that could have cost your team the championship.”

“It was so unfair, pal,” Jo said, “I swear, the coach risked losing the game by keeping you on the bench.”

“No doubt about it,” Jill added, “if he would’ve played you, the Pikes would have won by a larger margin.”

Miles sat up. “Think so? Thanks.”

Jo pulled into a doughnut shop. They ordered coffee and sat at a booth. Miles said, “Nice girlfriend I have! Bet Sheila has already moved on to some other guy.”

***

If Miles thought he was having a bad day, he should have walked a kilometre in Sheila’s shoes! She was with Tammy at the Kingston General Hospital, awaiting word on Bernice, their gravely ill mother. Tammy had come home from the asylum that afternoon to find her mom unconscious on the kitchen floor.

Bernice, or Bernie, as her friends called her, had baked a pan of hash brownies to welcome her daughter home. After removing the pan from the oven, she sampled a square—so rich and moist and chocolaty—one piece led to another until she devoured half the pan. She then had a seizure, which led to a heart attack!

A doctor approached Sheila and Tammy in the waiting room. "Sorry girls, we did everything we could. Your mother didn't make it."

That night, the Babcock sisters chanted requiems till dawn, stoned out of their gourds on Bernie's stupefying legacy, those wickedly delicious hash brownies.

***

Sheila and Tammy had their mother flown to New Orleans, where their aunt Olivia welcomed them with an open cape. Bernie Babcock was soon laid to rest, her coffin buried at a forty-five degree incline, so her corpse could overlook a black bayou, considered by her coven to be a hallowed medium to the *Otherworld.*

Olivia celebrated the unofficial adoption of her nieces with a séance. As the scent of cattails and reptiles emanated from the center of their candlelit circle, Bernie materialized with milky, cadaverous eyes, swamp weed entangled in her hair and black sediment caked upon her naked flesh. Like an aeolian harp, she moaned and howled to her daughters, "The spirit world has preordained one of thee a priestess; the other will soon reign with me in the nether regions of our sacred bayou."

***

Back at Perth Bay High, a rumour about Sheila's disappearance spread like tabloid wildfire (*Haven't you heard? Tammy escaped from the asylum and hacked her sister to pieces with an axe*!). After weeks of gruesome gossip, Miles hopped on his bike and headed for Rural Route #66. It was mild for mid March, early lamb weather. All that remained of winter's wrath looked like a random series of snow cones, scattered about dormant lawns and fields.

A realty sign had been staked beside Sheila's mailbox. As he cycled along the unkempt driveway, he reflected upon the time he walked Sheila home after school, last fall, when her smile made him feel ten feet tall, when holding her hand warmed his heart with beats heavy and proud—his sentimental musing burst like a bubble as the house came into view and he saw a scruffy fellow loading a pair of speakers into a pickup truck. Miles slammed on his brakes. The guy yelled up the road at him, "What are you doing here?"

"Why?" Miles snapped back, "What are *YOU* doing here?"

A second guy hauled a milk-crate full of albums out of the house. Miles recognized him as the bearded dude who had mocked his argyle socks, a few months ago at Sheila's party. They both dropped their loot and ran towards Miles, who turned his bike around and tore off. Half way up the driveway, he glanced over his shoulder: nobody followed. While his heartbeat slowed to its normal bike cruising pace, it sunk in that he'd never see Sheila Babcock, ever again.

But he was wrong: she visited that very night in his sleep. The dream began at a racetrack where hounds chased their own tails around while horses galloped after dangled carrots. Miles had to take a leak (he really did have to go: he'd downed a few beers before going to bed). He entered a washroom at the track, which turned out to be Sheila's bedroom.

She lay on her bed wearing nothing but a black cape, bodysuit and granny boots. Five strong men took turns touching her skin. Miles tried to walk away, but his knees buckled and he joined in. After all, there was still the ecstasy of her sexy, buxom body. The other men suddenly fled her bed, which was now set upon a stage, like when he saw the play, *Kiss Me Kate*. The audience watched as Sheila took his hand but looked away.

"Part of me will love you forever," he said.

"*No kidding*!" she said with a smirk hiking her deeply dimpled cheeks.

"May I hold you one last time?"

Despite her embrace, Miles awoke with a chill, laying in his skivvies beside a tangled heap of blankets. In desperate need of a pee, he rolled out of bed and staggered wearily to the washroom. While relieving himself forcefully through his semi-erect penis, he sensed his dream like an acid flashback, overshadowed by the aching void of having nobody to hold, once again, utterly single and alone.

Chapter Seventeen

Thanks to Harrietta and her private pleading in closed chambers, Dave was shellacked at every turn of his trial, the sessions dragging on for him like an endless, winless season—except when Laura appeared. Even though her testimony painted him as a vicious psychopath, her presence filled his heart with furious joy!

As a caged animal in jail, he was, of course, the king of beasts, his brutish size and reputation instantly wielding clout over fellow inmates. Nevertheless, he hated confinement in his 3X5 meter cell, a steel toilet near his feet as he slept upon a thin, flimsy mattress, laid upon an iron shelf bolted to a cement wall.

Worst of all, his letters to Laura went unrequited. Deeply disturbed by her estrangement, he played with his eye patch and stared, with his one good eye, at a razor sharp shank fashioned from a piece of pipe. On a hot night in June, after hours of morbid contemplation, he took his therapist's advice and gave poetry a try:

Dearest Sister,
Still not writing me back, eh? I understand. You have every reason to hate me. I'm giving poetry a try (how desparate am I?).

Missing My Sister

I once had a sister
on her heart,
I planted a blister
I went out of my mind
now she is blind.

I once had a freind

It came to an end

Gave him my wrath

In a bloodbath

I was crule and mean

Jealous and obsceen

Despite my sin

Are we not still ken?

Why should I live

unless you forgive?

Please stop your hate,

Before it's too late.

Before I'm barried in a field,

For God sakes Laura

take pity and yield!

Sincerely,

Dave

After Laura received his letter, she was about to tear it to pieces like all the others. But then she thought, *Am I the only one who can change*? She faced a prickly reality: their affair had started out consensually, she wanted him to touch her, at least in the beginning. She called Martha and asked her to read the letter. The trusty servant forced herself to be impartial, but felt like grabbing the blind beauty and shaking sense into her! When Laura heard the poem, she couldn't help feeling sorry for Dave.

That week, Harrietta accompanied Laura to the musical, *Jesus Christ Superstar*. Out of the hundreds who attended, only two sat comfortably in cotton sweatpants and running shoes. Throughout the show, Laura emphasized various themes by squeezing her mother's hand. Later, as they drove home, Laura said, "Wasn't it amazing, mom? Despite everything the Romans and Jews did to Jesus, he never held a grudge—he forgave everyone, even those who conspired to torture and murder him!"

"Laura, I get the feeling you've been trying to tell me something all evening."

"I think we should forgive Dave, give him a chance to redeem himself."

"Really?" Harrietta said in disbelief. "I lived with his father for over a decade. He was as vile and mean-spirited the day I met him, as he was when he took off on me! What makes you think Dave will be any different?"

"Because mom, he's getting help now, he's trying to change. Whereas dad never acknowledged his own faults, Dave is genuinely remorseful. According to his letter, he's wracked with so much guilt, he's become suicidal, in desperate need of forgiveness. Isn't that what Jesus taught us, to forgive?"

"Jeez Louise—you're full of surprises! Okay dear, I'll think about it."

"Mom, I hope you don't mind, but I already booked a visit on Sunday. Please don't make me go alone."

***

On Sunday afternoon, Laura and her mother sat on a steel bench, bolted to a cement wall, inside a cramped holding area where guests waited to see inmates. Harrietta shared awkward glances with two young women who wore halter tops and chain smoked between fits of foul language. One of them said, "Mike hates his know-it-all shrink and all his suck-ass bullshit! Only has to put up with him for another month."

Uh oh! Laura thought, *could Dave be playing the same game, going through the motions of therapy just for show? No, his poem was too desperate to be insincere.*

Harrietta whispered, "Laura, I'm not comfortable here. Could we cut our losses with Dave and leave—this place gives me the creeps!"

"Mom, we've come this far, let's give him a chance."

A guard ducked his head into the room and called out Laura and Harrietta's number. The two women followed the officer to a windowless room, where Dave jumped out of his chair to greet them. He was confused as to whether or not he should give them a hug. Harrietta shuttled Laura right passed him and sat her at a table.

As the ill-at-ease stepmother sat across from the convict, she was shocked by his clumpy haircut and pallid complexion, thought his eye-patch was a fitting accessory for his drab-green, prison uniform, like a ruthless pirate, doin' serious time for a heinous crime.

After an awkward silence, his lower lip trembled and he started to cry.

"It's alright Dave," Laura said. "This is difficult for all of us."

"Thank God you're here! It means a lot to me. But what's with the sweatpants? Did you guys come straight from a gym?"

"It's part of our new lifestyle," Laura said, "We now dress for health, comfort and movement."

"I have to admit, you both look good."

"You…look good too, Dave," Harrietta said, "all things considered, I mean."

"You don't have to lie, mom; but thanks just the same. Laura, what's this I've heard about your obsession with the sun? Is that really how you lost your sight?"

"Yes, I had a condition known as heliomania. But that's all behind me now."

"Laura, I'm *so* sorry about Norm. I lost my mind that night—literally! In fact, in my appeal, my lawyer wants me to change my plea to—actually, I'm not supposed to talk about that—point is, I honestly believed I was protecting your honour. Isn't that what big brothers are suppose to do? Through counselling, I've come to realize your private life was none of my business. Please forgive me."

"I forgive you Dave. It's time we moved on with our lives, I mean, me with mine and you with yours."

"Not completely separate, I hope."

"No, not completely." Something he once said popped into her head: *IT'S NOT OVER BITCH, UNTIL I SAY IT IS!*

"It can't be easy for you to get around, now that you're blind. When I get out of prison, I could be you're personal chauffeur."

"Nice of you to offer Dave, but I value my independence."

"Of course. Hey, do you still love shopping in Toronto?"

"Not anymore."

"What? You love shopping in TO. Once I get out of here, I could scoot you down the 401 any time you like."

"Thanks Dave, but that won't be necessary. So tell us about your therapy."

Dave slouched in his chair. He then asked Harrietta a series of questions, such as, *How's your car runnin'? Have you opened the pool yet?* And, *How's work going*? Surprised, Harrietta thought his sudden interest in her must have been part of his therapy.

Twenty minutes later, a burly guard opened the heavy steel door and said, "Time's up ladies."

Dave's eyes made a beeline for Laura. "I can't believe it's over already! Thanks for coming to see me. Please, come back again—any time you like."

Harrietta stood and said, "Dave, you need to be a model prisoner, so you can get out of here as soon as possible."

"Don't worry, mom—*I'll get out one way or another*."

Laura leaned across the table and whispered, "You really overplayed that cold shoulder routine, didn't you?"

Before he could respond, the guard escorted the two ladies out of the room.

Driving home, Harrietta said, "I don't think Dave has ever been so nice to me. Guess you were right, he's turning a new leaf. Too bad he can't go to the prom next week. Maybe I could pull some strings and—"

"Mom, we just made a huge mistake—he's been conning us!"

"What do you mean?"

"He's been nice to us because he's locked up and has no choice but to say things we want to hear. But then he showed his true colors when I turned down his offers to be my chauffer. That was when he vented his hostility by talking to you only, excluding me from the conversation entirely. Clearly, he hasn't changed one bit, probably won't stop hounding me until one of us ceases to exist."

***

Harrietta sat in Laura's room, brushing her thick, black hair. It was nearly time to leave for the prom. "As you know," the proud mother said, "I fully embrace your casual clothing philosophy. However, you only graduate from high school once. All the other girls will be wearing gowns and fancy shoes—"

"Mom—get real! When the dancing starts, the floor will be littered with all those 'fancy shoes' that murder feet, knees and vertebrae! As for those bulky, cumbersome gowns, well, I'm not about to walk around all night kicking the bottom of all that frivolous fluff!"

"Okay dear, I respect your decision. And anyway, what you're wearing is definitely a step up from sweatpants."

Her pert breasts were free to roam inside a white, cotton blouse; her hips and legs were unencumbered in a pair of khaki, rock-climbing pants; and her feet were well supported in a pair of black, soft-leather, hiking sandals, with soles cushioned well enough to walk a marathon!

***

When Harrietta and Laura entered the cafetorium, they faced an infestation of scrutiny, ranging from furtive glances, to shameless, eye bulging glares. Unflustered, the proud mother escorted her daughter to where Mercedes, Valerie and Wendy stood. Harrietta then left to retrieve refreshments, allowing the girls to catch up. After they said hi to each other, a hush filled the air between them. Eventually, Mercedes said, "*Nice outfit.*"

"Thanks," Laura said, ignoring the sarcasm. All three former friends used various excuses to leave her. Standing alone, the blind beauty listened to the wasp-like buzz of the crowd, until her mother returned with punch.

During dinner, Laura spoke, mostly to her mother, about music, meditation and exercise. When they finished eating, she could hardly wait for the awards ceremony to be completed, so she could jump onto the dance floor and release her pent up energy. To the cheers of the crowd, top jocks and scholarly types marched to the stage and accepted various accolades. When it was time for the parents to leave and let the young folks have their fun, Harrietta didn't budge.

"Don't worry about me mom, I'll be dancing the night away!"

"It's just that your friends have been ignoring you all evening and—"

"Mom, I'll be fine! If someone wants to be rude it's their problem! You said so yourself, graduation is a milestone. I'm determined to enjoy myself. Nobody can take this experience away from me. And who knows, I might even meet someone."

"Your spirit is indomitable! Okay dear, I'll be back to pick you up at midnight."

When Harrietta pushed her chair back, Laura latched onto her arm and said, "We've sure grown close lately, haven't we?"

"It's true, I cherish every second of our time together." She embraced Laura, then added, "You should have won an award tonight: *Most likely to survive*." She shared a laugh with her daughter, kissed her cheek, then left.

A DJ blasted "Brick House" by The Commodores. Laura said to anyone within earshot, "Would anybody like to dance?"

Hank Reddick, who sat at a nearby table, dodged in front of Tate Cooke to take Laura's hand. He led her to an open area of the dance floor, where the blind beauty had plenty of room to manoeuvre. Laura fused ballet and jazz moves, occasionally setting her hands on Hank's shoulders, thereby including him in her ecstatic expression of the song.

When "Brick House" ended, she asked Hank if he wanted to keep going. To the chagrin of his date, Hank agreed. The DJ played Peter Frampton's "Do You Feel Like We Do?" Hell yes, she felt those swanky guitar licks! To everyone's amazement, Laura dropped into the splits, bounced back to her feet, then spun three pirouettes. (Her roomy rock-climbing pants allowed her to move with unobstructed agility!)

Meanwhile, Hank's continuous two-step paled like a stickman drawn next to a Picasso! He raised his voice above the music, "Would you like some punch?"

"Okay, sure." Hank led her back to her seat. She assumed he'd return with refreshments but soon realized she was on her own again. With guidance from peers, she made her way to the punch bowl, where she smelled Valerie Doberman's rose scented perfume. "Hey Val, how's it going?"

"Fine."

"Did you settle on a university yet?"

"Yep."

Ignoring Valerie's curt rudeness, Laura focused on the lyrics of the current song "(Don't Fear) The Reaper." "Ever listen to the lyrics of this song, Val? The singer depicts death as a natural phase, nothing to be afraid of—romantic even—essential to eternal love. It's hauntingly beautiful."

"I never really listen to the words," Valerie said, "I go by the beat. "

Then, "***KA-BOOM***!" An explosion from the kitchen laid Laura flat upon her back with her ears ringing, buried beneath her former friend, who had buffered her from the blast. Laura could feel the heat of a wildly roaring fire. She heaved Valerie's lifeless body off her chest, sat up and tried to orientate herself.

Even that low to the ground, the smoke made her cough. She got to her feet but a fellow graduate, delirious with panic, knocked her back down. Nearby screams of agony intensified her terror. She charged forward on all fours, crawled over three bodies, then banged her head into a solid structure.

Dazed, she willed herself to remain conscious. She felt what she had banged into, found a knob and knew instantly she was before the doors beneath the stage. She let herself into the crawlspace and closed the door behind her. Being sheltered from the smoke eased her coughing to sporadic bouts.

Now what should I do? She wondered. *Perhaps there's a vent at the back, one I could escape through.* She wove and squirmed her way passed the props from last year's play, *Kiss Me Kate.* The wooden stage creaked and cracked from the pressure of the heat and she wondered if it would collapse upon her.

She made it to the back wall and felt cool cement-blocks but didn't find a vent. Nevertheless, she'd distanced herself from the smoke and heat. Safe for the moment, she realized how badly her head hurt, which led to a dizzy spell and nausea, causing her to faint.

When Laura awoke, she thought a paramedic was dabbing a wet cloth on the top of her head, cleaning a nasty abrasion there. But then she realized she was still under the stage, with some kind of rodent, likely a rat, licking her wound—she slapped the furry critter away!

Heat had infiltrated the crawlspace. She reached up and touched the stage floor: it was hot. *Where are the firemen*? She carefully re-examined the cement wall and found a thin, cool pipe, fixed in the corner between the wall and stage. *If I can bust this pipe, the water will cool the stage above me, prevent it from collapsing upon me*!

She searched the props and found a stray garden hoe, which she used to pry the pipe free, two of its brackets popping off the wall. She took a two handed grip on the pipe and bent it back and forth, back and forth.... After several strenuous moments, the copper kinked…and cracked—cold water sprayed upon her feverish body! With an overwhelming sense of relief, she thought *I'm gonna make it!*

As Laura sat in a cool pool of water, her mind began to wander, and she contemplated The Reaper song, the one she had listened to before the explosion. It occurred to her how sad it would be to die without a sense of "*Together in eternity*." She made up her mind to find everlasting love, if she survived.

A lifetime of hellfire seemed to pass when a section of the stage collapsed, about seven meters away from her—she heard voices—the firemen! One of them received a reprimand for walking on the stage before testing its integrity; it was his boot that had crashed through the floor.

Laura hollered for help! The firemen cleared a path wide enough to slide her out on a stretcher. In the ambulance, Harrietta held her daughter's hand and said, "I knew you should've won an award tonight."

Under the warm haze of opiates, Laura gazed quizzically.

"Most likely to survive, dear, you're the most likely to survive!"

Chapter Eighteen

On a Saturday morning in mid July, Jo awoke nestled between his two girlfriends. It occurred to him the only time he might have been more comfortable was when he was a fetus in his mother's womb. Patiently, he waited for Delores and Jill to awaken. The three lovers had bought a bungalow together shortly after Jo graduated from high school. Paying the mortgage was a cinch since all three cohabitants were gainfully employed.

Jo worked behind the customer-service counter of a Woolco department store. He was, of course, excellent at his job. Whenever complainants were crooks, like when thieves tried to return stolen goods for cash, Jo would expose their scams instantly. When grievances were legitimate, however, he'd appease the customers to such an extent, they often walked out of the store with additional merchandise tucked under their arms. (He thought his clairvoyance would best serve humanity in the secret service, a career move slated for November.)

Delores Petrie was a social worker, employed by The Children's Aid Society. Jo sensed she needed two lovers as a counterbalance, the weight of her daunting caseload offset by the heft of their threefold affection.

Jill Rigby worked in construction. Her foremen knew better than to perturb her with the task of twirling a stop/go traffic sign. Indeed, as a labourer with callused hands, or as a lover with a woman and a man, the brawny brunette thrived best as a physical animal.

Jo spooned Jill with the affection of a Greek god. When he planted a soft kiss upon her neck, just below her shortly cropped hair, his lax penis moved ever so slightly against her muscular buttocks. Meanwhile, Delores snuggled against Jo with her plentiful breasts pressed against his back, her leg draped over his thigh, her foot resting upon Jill's bulky calf muscle. Strands of her orangey-red hair were spread about her pillow, like lit fireworks in suspended animation.

Jo anticipated their Saturday morning rituals. First, they'd have a play fight. Then they'd make love. They made love a lot. If one of the trio was not in the mood but the other two started touching each other, it was inevitable that the reluctant one would succumb to the rapture. Like laughter, sexual fervour was contagious.

Finally, Jill stirred. Jo sensed she was thirsty. He slipped out of bed and dashed to the kitchen for orange juice. When he returned, Delores was stretching blissfully as her breasts were caressed by the amorous construction worker. Something told Jo they'd be skipping their play fight that morning.

***

After the enviable culmination of what began as thirty capable fingertips touching a trinity of erogenous zones, they jumped into the shower and practiced the extended version of you wash my back, I'll wash yours.

Shortly thereafter, the three famished lovers sipped freshly brewed coffee while preparing scrambled eggs, peameal bacon, hash browns and fruit salad. After eating, they packed camping gear and supplies into knapsacks. Whenever they had a weekend off together, they undertook an overnight outing. Two weeks ago, they canoed to a remote island on Lake Ontario. Before that, they hiked in Algonquin Park.

Today's activity was chosen by Jill. When she was a little girl, her great-grandfather, a Mohawk Chief, told her about a secret cave painting half way down a cliff, on the Mill River Escarpment. The threesome planned to meditate and camp amid the intrigue of Jill's ancient, ancestral artwork.

"I'll call Miles one last time," Jo said.

"We haven't seen him since he started working," Delores said. "The four of us used to have a lot of fun together, he was like a kid brother to us."

"I think it's great he found a job," Jill said, "but he seems to be taking it too seriously. Does he plan to be a fish gutter for the rest of his life?"

Jo dialed his cousin's number and let it ring several times. Just as he was about to hang up, a gruff voice answered, "Hello?"

"Miles, is that you?"

"Huh?"

"Hey Pal, did I wake you?"

"Oh, Jo, yes you did wake me. But I'm glad you did. I slept through my alarm. Have to get to work. Guess I'll skip my shower this morning."

"When I called last night, Betty said you were working your fifth, consecutive overtime shift. Are you into slave labour, or what?"

"Only make minimum wage Jo, need all the overtime I can get. Besides, fish gutters don't ask questions, we just show up for our shifts and slit the fish." Miles yawned, then said, "Did you hear the latest about the 'prom bomb'?"

"I read in the Whig Standard, the police don't have a single lead."

"Sure glad I didn't let Betty talk me into going. I didn't want to be around coach O'Reilly, or any of my teammates, not after the incident at the pub."

"I was lucky too, Miles. Almost let Delores and Jill talk me into going. But I knew people wouldn't approve of us; it would have been tiresome listening to malicious thoughts all night. Did you make it to the funerals of your teammates?"

"Yes, it was horrible to see their families suffer like that. What a strange twist of fate: Hank, Art and Tate were on top of the world following the championship game—now, they're no longer of this world."

"So Miles, is there any way I can convince you to join us today?"

"I already told you, I have to work."

"You're always working! Come on Pal, take the weekend off. You won't regret it. The girls miss you; they'd love you to join us."

"Nice of you three to think of me, but I'm making money for the first time in my life and I like it! As Betty always says, *a man has to earn a living*."

"I realize having a job is important, but it's okay to live a little too. Besides, you'll burn out if you keep working this much overtime. Come be a cave dweller with us—we'll have a riot! How about it Coz?"

"Nah, you guys go ahead. I'll take a rain check."

"If it rains, there's no point in camping! Come on Miles, call in sick."

"What? I can't do that! Man, I never thought I'd say this, but you're becoming a bad influence!"

"Okay Miles, I respect your decision. Just remember: you can always make more money, but you can never make more time."

"If I hustle, I can still make it to work on time—" ("Click.")

Jo couldn't get over it. Was Miles really putting fish guts ahead of fresh air, sunny skies, and a mysterious cave? Perhaps it was just a phase.

As Miles cycled to Murphy's Fish Factory, he thought about the real reason he stayed away from his cousin. It drove him crazy that Jo maintained a vibrant relationship with two women when Miles himself slept alone every night. The only way to conceal his resentment from the wily clairvoyant was to stay away from him entirely. The estrangement tore Miles up inside, so he took it out on the slaughtering tables.

There was one other reason Miles worked his guts out, gutting fish: he aspired to get rich through the magic of compound interest, a concept he had recently learned from his father. Except for the nominal fee he paid Betty each month, Miles saved every cent he earned, quickly growing his bank account.

Later that day, just before lunch, Miles sliced open his thumb. While a secretary dressed his wound at her desk, their foreman, whose hairy forearms seemed to confirm humans evolved from apes, burst into her office and said to Miles, "Don't expect to be paid for clumsiness—I'm docking you an hour's pay!"

***

Equipped with sleeping bags, knotted climbing rope, food rations, bottled water, and wineskins, Jo, Delores and Jill pedaled their bikes on a path that ran along the top of the Mill River Escarpment. Jo wondered what Jill meant when she hollered, "OLE—OLE!" Then he noticed a sign on an old, decrepit barn: “BEWARE OF BULL.” Damn, he thought, today of all days, I had to wear a red T-shirt!

After three hours of clipping through the forest, they decided to break for lunch. Upon a cliff overlooking the river, they set up a picnic. Jo said to Jill, “Will you jump off the cliff before or after lunch?”

“Jesus Jo, am I that predictable? I’m jumping before I eat. Don’t want to get a cramp in the water.” She stripped naked.

“Guess you’ll climb down first,” Delores said, “to make sure it’s safe.”

Jill borrowed Jo’s binoculars and scanned below. “Looks safe to me.”

“We’re only about four stories high,” Jo said, “The worst you’d probably do is break a leg.”

“*Thanks for the vote of confidence*!” Jill said. She fastened their rope around an oak tree, then threw the lose end over the edge. Without counting to three, without second guessing herself whatsoever, she charged the cliff and jumped as high as she could into the blue sky… “KER-SPLASH!” She disappeared beneath the current.

Jo and Delores dropped to the ground and peeked over the edge. Panic seized their hearts when Jill didn’t surface. But then her head bobbed above the water. “YOWWW—WHAT A RUSH!” she hollered up, “What are you two landlubbers waiting for? The water’s beautiful!”

Reluctantly, Jo and Delores undressed. He could sense she was as petrified as he was. Before long, they were standing at the top of the cliff with a summer breeze goose-bumping their naked flesh. Despite Jill clucking at them like a mad chicken, neither Jo nor Delores were close to jumping. Then, Jill yelled, "THE BULL—THE BULL IS COMING—JUMP—JUMP—NOW!"

She was too far away for a telepathic read. Bushes along the cliff rustled. Jo and Delores looked at each other with gaping eyes—THE BULL! They stepped back a couple of paces, squeezed each other's hand, then bolted over the edge—"AHHHHHHH—KER/KER-PLUNK/PLUNK!" Their combined impact registered on Jill's personal Richter scale. Jo and Delores surfaced amid waves of post-terror exhilaration.

They looked up, expecting to see a mean-eyed bull huffing down at them; no such beast appeared. Jo sensed mischief quelling in Jill. He said to her, "You can only see the edge of the cliff from down here; how could you have seen a bull charging?"

"*Bull indeed!* The barn we passed was dilapidated, obviously abandoned for years. But let's face it: the two of you were never going to jump without a little, extra incentive."

"If there was no bull," Delores said, "what was coming at us?" They looked up and saw a grey squirrel scurry across the edge of the cliff.

"*Toro, Toro my dears*," Jill said between fits of laughter.

Jo and Delores splashed her as they all treaded water. They then dunked her twice, though it wasn't easy, the brawny construction worker was so damn strong! Exhausted by mirthful exertion, but still half laughing, they swam to shore and collapsed upon a patch of grass.

After a brief rest, the trio scaled the cliff to where they could reach the knotted rope. Climbing one at a time, Delores went first. Staring up at her, Jill said, "Look Jo, a *Moon Camel*!"

Through his clairvoyance, he knew she was referring to Delores's camel toe, beneath her moon. "I suppose if you were looking up at me you'd call it a *Moon Rat*!"

They both laughed so hard, Delores yelled down, "What's so funny?" Jo said they'd explain over lunch. When she was about three quarters of the way up, Delores hollered, "You'll have to be careful here: there's a thicket of thorn bushes."

Once she was at the top, it was Jill's turn to climb. "No laughing at my Moon Camel!" she said.

"No promises! Then again, why would I laugh at something so beautiful?"

She kissed him, then pulled herself up the rope.

When they were all safe and sound at the top of the cliff, they made good use of their first-aid kit, doctoring each other's cuts and scraps, inflicted by the brush like nature's barbed wire. While Jill dabbed iodine upon the side of Jo's buttock, she said, "If I didn't know better, I'd say this scratch happened during the heat of passion!"

They dressed, ate a small lunch, packed up, then resumed their journey along the path. Four hours later, Jill squeezed her hand brakes and came to a stop. "See that rock, the one that looks like the head of a tomahawk? That's the landmark my great-grandfather told me about." She hopped off her bike and led them to the face of the escarpment, where they crawled to the edge and looked down.

"There's the ledge!" Delores said.

Jill tied one end of their rope to the bottom of a stout maple tree, then tossed the remaining coil over the edge. One by one, they climbed down to their newly found balcony. They stepped inside the cave, shined flashlights and were astounded! "So, it's true!" Jill said, "This is the cave painting my great-grandfather told me about!"

The scene depicted three voluptuous women raising their hands towards various celestial objects, including seven stars, two fuzzy patches of nebula and a comet. "I get the feeling there's a specific message in the painting," Jo said.

"A nebula is a nursery for stars," Delores said, "Perhaps the women are worshipping creation."

"I don't know about that," Jill said, "Would ancient, native women have known stars are born in a nebula?"

"They would if they were aliens!" Jo said.

Jill laughed. "You watch too much *Star Trek*!"

Delores revised her theory: "Perhaps they were simply appreciating the beauty of the heavens."

"You might be right," Jo said, "The night sky was a much brighter canvas before electricity was invented. Nowadays, much of the cosmos is obliterated from the naked eye by oceans of light pollution."

"Are you sure about that, Jo?" Jill said, "Whenever we go camping like this, the night sky seems jammed packed with stars."

"It's true we can see more when we're away from the city. But imagine what it was like when there was no artificial light whatsoever. A cluster of brilliant blue stars would've sparkled like sapphires upon black velvet. Perhaps the rings of Saturn could've been seen with the naked eye."

"The cave has already stoked our imaginations," Jill said, "This will be an excellent place to meditate."

Jo and Delores agreed. But first, they needed sustenance. While the umbra of dusk fell across the river, the merry threesome used wineskins to toast their "exceptional expedition." They then cracked open Tupperware and ate cheese, bread and various salads.

When it was dark, they sat upon a blanket beneath the stars. Then came the deep breathing and transcendent state of calm. About an hour later, Jill was the first to open her eyes. She waited patiently for her two lovers to resurface. When they did, she said, "I have something to share, something so extraordinary, I hope I can find the words to describe it!

"Deep into my meditation, I was overwhelmed by a sense of *déjà vu*, and a sort of portal opened in my mind, prompted by the night sky, and it gave me a strong sense of us in the infinite universe. I then realized this can't possibly be the only time we've camped on this cliff because everything has happened before, and will reoccur, over and over again for all eternity!"

Delores raised her eyebrows. "There's just one thing I don't understand and that's *everything you just said*!"

Jo said to Jill, "Are you saying *déjà vu* is a sense of ourselves in the infinite universe, which implies we've been here before, and will be again, in other lifetimes perhaps?"

"I swear Jo, it's like you can read my mind!"

"I still don't understand," Delores said.

"Let me try to explain further," Jill said, "Suppose I claimed another version of us will be sitting here again in two hundred years. Well, that wouldn't be likely; too many things would have to reoccur in that timeframe. For example, we'd all have to be reborn, we'd have to meet each other again, have to know about this cave, then find it, etc.. It's highly unlikely the chain of events that brought us here this evening, will happen again in a mere couple hundred years, at this exact location.

"*If,* however, I increase the timeframe to billions of years and expand the distance to cover billions of galaxies, then our recreation would be more likely, because the events that led us here would have more time and space, more opportunities to reoccur.

"Now, here's the kicker: billions of galaxies, over billions of years, is a brief speck compared to infinity! Without limitations to time or space, it becomes inevitable the long chain of events that brought us here will reoccur; in other words, the sequence that made us happen has forever and wherever to repeat itself—therefore it'll keep happening for certain, for all eternity! Not on this exact planet per se, but on one exactly like it, *out there somewhere*."

"If I understand you correctly," Jo said, "a replica of us has always been at this cave and always will be."

"Exactly, Jo! Somewhere out there, in infinite space, the three of us are sitting in an identical fashion, coming to these very same conclusions. Other instances will happen in the future, others have already occurred in the past."

"So," Delores said with bright green eyes, "The infinite universe is like a giant maze of mirrors, some reflecting replicas of itself over vast quantities of space; others reflecting in sequence, over eons of time."

"Excellent metaphor!" Jo said, "And what a paradox! Although our individual, physical selves will die one day, we live forever, elsewhere…and so death is not the end of anything but part of an eternal cycle."

"Holy smokes," Jill said, "I just realized something else: we don't need anything magical or spiritual to live forever—it happens naturally."

"I see what you mean," Jo said. "Regardless of our beliefs, raw infinity makes us all immortal."

Jill noticed Delores was crying. "What's the matter sweetie?"

"My kid brother Danny, who died of leukemia. I miss him so much. But now I see us clearly, on a sunny day at our favourite park, together forever in the infinite universe, climbing monkey bars, happy as larks!"

Jo and Jill slung an arm around her. He said, "That brawny construction worker sure has some mighty deep thoughts, eh Delores?"

"Credit where credit is due, Jo," Jill said, "Before I met you, I didn't know the difference between a quark and a quasar!"

"It's true," Delores said, "You're like a walking encyclopedia!"

"Thanks ladies, the two of you are too kind. I think I've figured out the cave painting."

"Oh? Do tell," Jill said.

"Perhaps the artist was comparing the beauty of women to the heavenly bodies above. I find it inspirational." And with that, he pulled a journal and pencil out of his knapsack, turned on a flashlight and began writing.

While Jo jotted down his thoughts, the trio passed the wineskin around and shared stories about lost loved ones. Their discussion led to a pact, sealed with tender kisses, to make the most of their precious time together.

Jo then said, "I've finished my poem. It could use more polishing, but in the spirit of spontaneity, I'll lay it on you right here, right now:

"In Delores Petrie, I see
Vermillion hair like a solar flare
And amazing, emerald-green eyes
Enigmatic and magnetic
As borealis in the night skies
Her kisses feel like solar wind
Warmth of the sun upon our skin

In Jillian Rigby, I see
Chiselled and rugged good looks
A Jovian eloquence
Other worldly olive skin
Lit by the hue of two blue stars
Aligning us in time and in space
Willed by the wont of her warm embrace

"Indeed," he added, "when I look at the two of you, the awesome beauty of the universe is exemplified right here before me!"

As the two young women eased Jo onto his back and removed his clothes, their thoughts astonished him. Not only were they thrilled by his poem; but also, they were jealous of each other's verse, their competitive juices stirred soaking wet! They had always performed oral sex in triangular formations—until now—this was the first time both girls went down on him together.

Amid their ravenous licking, sucking and lip smacking, Jo stroked their hair, looked up at the stars, and perceived with perfect clarity, he had always been at the cave that amazing night and always will be—for all eternity!

Chapter Nineteen

Miles was so overtired, having Sunday off didn't come close to recharging his batteries. At least he wouldn't have to ride his bike to work in the morning. One of Anton's colleagues sold Miles a 1970, lime-green Datsun for four hundred bucks.

The lanky eighteen year old went to bed shortly after dinner and was just drifting off to sleep when Betty yelled, "MILES—PHONE!"

He dragged himself to the living room where his mother carped at him for going to bed without saying "goodnight." In the middle of a vigorous yawn, he spoke into the receiver, "Hello?"

"Miles! It's Jo. I have to tell you about our weekend—it was magnificent!"

Half asleep, Miles heard fragments of Jo's ravings: "Beware of bull…. Jumped off the cliff…. Cave painting…. See the rings of Saturn with the naked eye…. A billion galaxies…. Infinite time and space…. *Death is not the end of existence*!"

"Fascinating, Jo. So did you guys *do it* in the cave?"

"Miles! I just gave you proof our existence is eternal and all you want to talk about is sex? Haven't you ever wondered about an afterlife?"

"I'm struggling with the life I'm in!"

"Okay Pal, I understand. You've been working so many hours, you're exhausted. We'll talk again when you're caught up on sleep."

"That might not be for a while. I'm working another double shift tomorrow."

***

True to his word, Miles worked sixteen hours on Monday. He was so burned out, the day went by in a blur, his mind blanking out blocks of time, like a trucker with white-line fever, oblivious to gaping stretches of highway.

As he drove home in his "new" late model Datsun, his eyelids felt like heavy padlocks locking—his forehead bounced off the steering wheel! I'm tilted in a ditch, he thought as his eyes blinked open again, driving in a ditch?—WAKE UP! He cranked the steering wheel left and levelled the car back onto the road. With his heart pounding in his throat, he thought, only a few more miles to go. Albeit, dark, lonely miles.

His doors suddenly locked with a clunk. *Power locks in this old crate?* he thought. But there were no switches. He pulled on the door lock knob…it wouldn't budge. The steering wheel suddenly had the feel of ceasing steel. He slammed on the brakes but they seemed to bleed out beneath his heel. Aimed at a house beyond a stop sign, Miles braced himself for impact—at the last second, his car handled like a Ferrari, whipping around the corner with a slight fishtail!

Okay, I've lost it, he thought, gone completely insane! The possessed Datsun pulled into an empty parking lot. He wondered why it stopped at Queen's University. Four jacks jumped out of the trunk and positioned themselves under the car. *Up, up and away*—the carjacks self-replicated, one upon another. Before long, the Datsun was an obstacle for crows! He looked down below, through the side window, and saw a mad bull bucking and charging in circles.

The windshield then seemed like a giant magnifying glass as stars clustered ever closer. When the carjacks finally stopped replicating, the lime-green auto swayed in the wind, as if waving to Saturn. The golden planet's icy rings, like crystalline highways, reflecting sunlight so brightly, Miles reached into his glove box and donned a pair of sunglasses.

Though astounded by the amazing view, he felt crushed by a tidal wave of exhaustion, as if falling asleep within a dream. Before he slipped away, a delicate voice said, "The choice is yours, of course; but you could also choose to stay and see the light of another day."

A young woman, with distinctly symmetrical features, appeared in the passenger seat. Her golden blond hair fell well beyond her shoulders. She wore a silky white, see-through gown. He looked away from her breasts, the shape of two perfectly formed lemons. "Apparently," he said, "There's beauty in the universe even greater than women."

"Perhaps; but in your experience, has there been anything better than loving them?"

He nodded towards the windshield. "Too many dark, empty spaces out there."

"Love will fill the void if you strive towards a greater purpose."

"I have a great purpose! Are you familiar with the magic of compound interest?"

"So your goal is to slave and save while living with Betty indefinitely. This makes sense to you?"

"Eventually, I'll be rich—livin' the American dream!"

"If you limit your dreams to money, you'll stagnate and die inside. Why do you think I brought you to the university?"

"But the universe is closing in on me faster than I can bear!" He smelled burnt popcorn, then faded to black. When his eyes blinked open, she was resuscitating him mouth to mouth. Despite his sense of doom, or maybe because of it, he kissed her, and when the tip of her tongue touched his, a shockwave jolted his heart like a lightning rod ignited with white hot sparks—

"*CLEAR*!" a paramedic shouted before zapping Miles a second time with a defibrillator. To the rescuers' relief, his heart resumed the inertia of a steady beat. His universe had indeed shrunk: firemen were forced to use the Jaws of Life to cut him out of the wreckage. He suffered broken ribs, a collapsed lung and substantial blood loss.

While paramedics loaded him into an ambulance, Miles groaned, "I'm hurtin' all over!"

"No worries, Pal," one of them said. "The morphine will kick in any second."

"*Whoa, I saw Saturn's golden glow / Outside my car window / An angel up there, with golden hair / Dared me to dream / Beyond my money scheme / She warded off death / With the air of her healing breath...*"

The paramedic looked at his partner. "Who do we have here? *Shakespeare*?"

Laughing, his partner said, "This young man needs a CAT scan!"

Chapter Twenty

After seven months of rehab, Miles returned to the fish factory, but only worked part time, so he could attend three courses at St. Lawrence College. His language skills grew by leaps, thanks to the trifurcated tutoring of his aunt, uncle and cousin.

Work and studies kept him so busy, the spring/summer semester passed in a flash. Then came the anticipatory anxiety of waiting for his final grades to arrive in the mail. Two weeks later, he opened the college stationery and could hardly believe his eyes: two As and a B+, nearly straight As! To celebrate, he took Ana, Igor and Jo out for dinner at Aunt Lucy's Restaurant.

Brimming with a new found confidence, he applied to Queen's University as a mature student…and was accepted! Thus came an end to his toil as a fish gutter.

His former colleagues held a farewell party for him on the Saturday of the Labour day weekend. Miles locked his bike outside the mongers' favourite pub, The Port's Pier. When he approached the gang inside, Harry, their furry, bulky foreman, said, "There he is, the *edge-u-ma-cated* one!"

"Hey fellas," Miles said, beaming with pride, "Thanks for coming everyone, this is great!"

Harry's brother, Fred, said, "Any excuse to get drunk will do!" He poured Miles a glass of draft beer. They all chanted, "CHUG-CHUG-CHUG." Miles obliged them and they all cheered. Another monger, Wiry John, said to Miles, "So what degree did you get at college?"

"I didn't get a degree; I attended college to prepare myself for university."

“Oh,” John said, “so what did you study?”

“I took two English courses, as well as Intro to Philosophy.”

“Philosophy, eh,” Fred said, “What do you learn in a course like that?”

“That philosophers love to argue! For example, some believe in dualism, the notion there’s a spirit separate from the body. But a growing number of neuroscientists argue there’s nothing beyond brain matter, no such thing as a soul.”

“What do you think?” Harry said, “Are we a bunch of soulless bastards or what?”

From an A+ essay he’d written about eternal existence, inspired by Jill’s revelation at the cave, Miles paraphrased: “I believe the cyclical nature of matter renders a so called ‘soul’ as superfluous and therefore nonexistent.”

They all had a look on their faces that said, “Huh?”

Miles offered an example: “Let’s say someone dies and is buried in a field. A hundred years later, a farmer plants corn over the grave. The physical stuff that used to be a human being has rotted into the soil and absorbed by the crop. Part of the corpse has thus transformed into corn.

“Now, if somebody eats the corn, then nature has come full circle because the person who had been buried in the field is now physically part of whoever has consumed the corn. There’s no need for mysterious spirits, or a soul to explain how humans are reincarnated. Nature is self-replicating. There’s something in philosophy known as Occam’s razor—”

“SO!” Fred interrupted, “You think we all come back as corn! This is why you spent the big bucks to go to school—TO LEARN WE TURN INTO CORN!”

Harry added, “Now I know what they mean when they say ‘*He comes from good stalk*!’”

The fish gutters laughed so hard, Miles couldn’t help but join in. When they finally settled down, he said, “Guess that’s why I’m going back to school, because there’s so much I need to find out.”

Wiry John raised his glass: “I’ll drink to that!”

The topic changed to their full breasted secretary, Dita, something about the time Fred and another employee, Burt, walked in on her while she was adjusting her pantyhose. Indeed, the male employees would use any excuse to duck into her office. After consuming eyefuls of her, they’d return to the slaughtering tables with invigorated zeal. Miles often wondered if old man Murphy had hired her simply to boost the morale of the mostly male staff. In any event, he had heard these sorts of stories a hundred times.

Besides boredom, Miles felt a deepening divide from his former workmates. Their mockery of his theory, on *Natural Reincarnation*, seemed to confirm a hostility he’d been sensing for months now, as if many of them resented him for going back to school. By ten o’clock, he felt compelled to leave, feigned going to the washroom, then bailed out the back door.

As he cycled through the crisp, late August air, the wind blew the smoky bar stench out of his long, flowing hair. He activated a light on the front of his bike, veered off the asphalt and headed down a dirt road. He stopped at the quarry, where he had parked with Vanessa, the girl he met at a party, the first girl he ever went down on. Reflecting upon that night, he thought, *Those were the days*!

Looking at the water he thought, impromptu biathlon! Under a crescent moon, he stripped naked and jumped off a rock, into a pool of reflected starlight. The water was cold but cycling had stoked his internal furnace, a warmth he maintained with a hearty breaststroke.

When he was half way across the quarry, car lights flashed over his head. Wondering who had joined him, he swam a U–turn and saw somebody was building a fire near his bike. He reached the shore and propped his chest upon a rock ledge.

The flickering flames revealed two women who shared an obvious family resemblance, surely a mother and daughter. The younger lady, who, for some reason wore sunglasses in the dark, said to him, "You'll be cold coming out of the water. Why don't you warm up by our fire?"

"Sounds good." It occurred to him he was talking to the most beautiful young woman in the country! He'd never seen her dressed like this before: she wore grey sweatpants, running shoes and a jean jacket. With his shivers growing evermore convulsive, he uprooted a shrub and climbed out of the water. He then altered his "fig leaf" from the front of his body to the rear, depending on their line of vision. He dressed, then sat beside Laura and her mother, on a log long enough to seat all three of them.

"Your lips look blue," Harrietta said. "Let's wrap this around your shoulders." She shrouded him in a cozy comforter, then poured tea from a thermos. As the plastic cup warmed his hands, he thanked Harrietta, then introduced himself.

The Needler ladies returned the courtesy. He said to Laura, "You probably don't remember me but we went to the same high school."

"Your last name seems familiar, Miles. Have we met?"

"I don't think we've had the pleasure." (He saw no benefit in mentioning their only interaction, when she bit his head off for bumping into her, after Dave had pushed him in their school's cafeteria.) "Um, this tea hits the spot. Sure was cold coming out of the water. Lucky you kind ladies came along when you did."

While Harrietta explained their recent tendency to explore new sensations, such as the nocturnal serenity of the quarry, Laura remembered Jo Martini's letter, the one that exalted her as a beautiful princess, whisking through a forest upon a magnificent steed. And while the fire warmed the front of her body beneath the stars, the passion, *oh so palpable* in Jo's poem, deflected right to Miles, and she longed to embrace him and plaster his face with loving, lambent kisses. "The fire is dying down, Miles," she said, "Would you mind gathering more wood for us?"

He borrowed their flashlight and headed into the forest. Laura whispered to her mother, "Alright mom, you can leave us now. I won't be too late."

"Are you crazy?" Harrietta said, "I'm not leaving you in the forest with a stranger!"

"It's okay mom, I knew his cousin in high school. These guys are perfect gentlemen."

"He does seem well mannered." Harrietta chuckled and added, "I couldn't help noticing when he came out of the water—he has a nice butt!"

"Mother—you're terrible!" They shared a laugh together.

Miles returned with his arms forklifting a load of wood. Harrietta bid the young couple farewell, then drove away in her Mercedes.

"Your mother's nice."

"Thanks. So what do you do when you're not swimming quarries in the night?"

He told her about his scholarly pursuits and they discussed the philosophical implications of existentialism, relative to what she had learned from Dr. May. Laura then said, "Besides developing your intellect, what else do you want out of life?"

"Well, to be honest, I'm hoping to find a meaningful relationship. If I'm lucky, it'll be with someone as beautiful as you…gee, did I say that out loud? Hope you don't mind."

"I don't mind at all. Thanks for the compliment. What do you mean by 'a meaningful relationship'?"

"I could sum it up with something I wrote last year in an English course. (She nodded approval.) Our assignment was to turn a life experience into an analogy. This is what I came up with: One cold day in February, I was having a shower and ran out of hot water. As I dried off, I realized my clothes were downstairs in the dryer. Shivering, I wrapped a towel around myself and headed for the basement. My parents kept the thermostat set low to save on fuel bills, so our house was freezing!

"I hustled to the laundry room and pulled on a sweater, still warm from the dryer. I never appreciated warmth like that before—not until tonight when you and your mother shared your fire. Here was my analogy: connecting with someone, in a meaningful relationship, is like slipping into a warm sweater—it provides cozy insulation from an otherwise frigid, indifferent world."

"That's sweet, Miles. Would you mind if I touched your face?"

"Go ahead." As she used all ten fingertips to feel his eyebrows, cheeks, nose, lips and chin, goose bumps spread from the back of his head to the bottom of his spine.

"Chiselled," she said, "Sharply defined. I'd guess you're slim and fit."

"You know that from touching my face?"

"Actually, you did ride your bike here to go for a swim, so it's not difficult to figure out you're in good shape. It's amazing though, what you can tell about a person by touching their features. You try it."

The thought of touching her made his heart pound. He started by running his fingers through her thick, black hair, which felt even softer than it looked. He removed her sunglasses, then felt around her enigmatic eyes and prominent cheek bones. When he touched her lips, she took two of his fingertips and slipped them into her mouth! Caught off guard by her sensual spontaneity, a shockwave of ecstasy took his breath away. She nestled her cheek into the palm of his hand and said, "I don't live far, just across Salem's bridge. Would you like to walk me home?"

"I'd love to." As Laura tucked her teacup and blanket into a beach bag, Miles filled the empty thermos with quarry water and made the embers of the fire sizzle like sauna rocks. She grasped his elbow and he lit the path with the light on his bike, which he rolled along with his free hand.

When they passed the spot where Jo was found naked, beaten and catatonic, Miles sensed horror like a haunting echo of muted screams. As shadows amid the trees grew deeper and darker, a chill ran down his spine. "You've suddenly gone quiet," Laura said, "Is everything alright?"

"The forest…is so still." They stopped to listen.

"Like the phrase," she said, "*In the dead of night*. Sort of spooky."

They strolled farther up the path, to where trickling water broke the silence of the forest. Halfway across Salem's Bridge, Laura stopped and said, "Listen to the babble of the brook… sounds random, yet rhythmic…like jazz music."

"Like jazz music?" He listened intently. "Whoa, good ear! I hear what you mean: it's fluttery yet fluid and steadfast…like how you make my heart beat." They latched onto each other and kissed without coyness, their tongues bridging massive gaps of loneliness and yearning.

She suddenly pulled away. "You're shivering." She touched his hair. "No wonder: you're still a bit wet. Come on, my house is close. I'll warm you up again with another fire."

When they reached the Needler mansion, Miles said, "Whoa, this place is palatial! Does the Queen stay here when she visits Canada?"

"Thanks Miles; but, the most important thing about a home isn't its size but its warmth."

"You mean like the incredible warmth I've been feeling from you all evening?"

Laura smacked a kiss upon his cheek and they went inside.

A short while later, Miles was cocooned in a luxurious white robe, nestled with Laura on a sofa before a lit fireplace. When he sipped fine wine, (gamey tasting with a hint of cherry), he had the uncanny sense he was dreaming. He pinched himself and waited…still there—this was really, really, really happening!

"I've made a compilation tape," Laura said, "Hope you like it." She pressed a button on a remote. The first song was "Romeo and Juliet," by Dire Straits. When Mark Knopfler sang, "*Juliet, the dice was loaded from the start / And I bet and you exploded in my heart*," Laura reached into Miles's borrowed robe and felt his heavy heartbeat while caressing his chest.

Next, Kate Bush belted "Feel It." "*God, but you're beautiful aren't you? / Feel your warm hand walking around / I won't pull* away...." Miles kissed Laura and slid his hand along her inner thigh…she parted her legs slightly and he brushed against her sweet spot, ever so lightly, almost as if by chance.

When Rod Stewart sang "Tonight's the Night," Miles said, "I love this song! It was my favourite back in high school."

"His raspy voice is so *Ooh la, la*," Laura said amid heavy breaths.

Miles swigged a belt of wine and flooded her mouth while French kissing. With the tip of his tongue, he followed a trickle from the corner of her lips, down her cheek and onto her neck. Though he'd never given a hickey before, he lit like a Vampire, instinctively, and grew a purply blue hue upon her flesh.

She pulled off her top and he ravished her perky, bare breasts, licking and sucking her nipples, till they were hard as bullets between his lips. She then parted his robe and his erection practically jumped out at her.

He tugged off her sweatpants, panties and socks, then kissed north from her ankle…passed her knee…along her inner thigh…then he planted his tongue into her wetness. She slipped her fingers into his hair, gently lifted his head, and said, "I'd definitely like to try that some time; for now, I just want to feel you inside me, if that's okay."

"*If* that's okay?" He had to laugh. Without further ado, Miles obliged her. Upon sinking her fingernails into his fleshy rear end, she thought, mother was right, *he does have a nice butt*!

Like an Alpine yodeler who slips on a patch of moist moss and plummets off a cliff, he released so many prolonged, primal groans, Laura was able to jump off to meet him with a climax of her own! "Sorry about that" he said, panting "It's been such a long time for me and you're so beautiful and you feel so amazing."

"It's okay Miles, I came too. And your orgasm felt wonderful—didn't think you were ever going to stop!"

He buried his face in her hair and smelled remnants of night air mixed with her natural essence. "Uh, I can keep going…if you want me to."

"*If* I want you to?" she had to laugh.

He thrust deeply, slowly and steadfastly for as long as she needed this time, though she didn't need long. Her second climax gained momentum like a tidal wave upon rapids, catapulting her over the edge of a waterfall. She whispered, "*OH-MY-GOD—OH-GOD—OH-GOD—O-H-H-H-H-H* ***my god***!" It was the first time he felt divine and it was good! After her mighty O, she gasped—dying of sensitivity—but held on as he came again, his second orgasm nearly as earth shattering as his first. As her vital signs panted back to normal, a tear streamed down her cheek.

"Did I do something wrong, Laura?"

"Are you kidding?"

"Then why are you crying?"

"I just really needed that, Miles. Thanks."

"You're thanking me? No problem, my pleasure—literally my pleasure!"

They cuddled beneath a blanket while listening to side two of Laura's tape; both fell asleep to a Beatles' song, George Harrison singing, "*Something in the way she moves / Attracts me like no other lover...*"

In a dream like a time machine, Miles travelled back to Murphy's Fish Factory, where his coworkers squeezed into Dita's office; only it wasn't the full busted secretary on her knees pleasing the entire male staff, but Sheila! Miles awoke in her bed. She slept with her back to him. *This can't be happening*! he panicked, *Must return to quarry*! She didn't move when he jumped out of her bed. Was she even breathing?

Naked, he bolted out the front door and a gang of bikers poured out of the house after him. He tried to run but his legs felt heavy as stone. Looking over his shoulder, he saw a bearded guy twirling a mace. Before the spiked ball could crush his skull, Miles willed himself free of gravity—up, up and away—above telephone poles and the tallest trees, the wind blowing his hair and manhood every which way. But the will to fly, fuelled by frantic dream logic, exhausted him and he quickly lost altitude, crash landing…

…as if through the roof of the Needler mansion. Awakened by his own pounding heartbeat, he seemed to have landed right behind Laura, spooning her tenderly. As it sunk in he no longer had anything to do with Sheila, relief overwhelmed him like opium. Comforted by Laura's cozy warmth, his heartbeat synchronized with her deep sleep breathing, sedating him into his own blissful slumber.

Chapter Twenty-one

Two years flew by for Miles like a magic carpet ride. Not only had he maintained a solid B+ average at Queen's; but also, he spent nearly every spare moment with his gorgeous girlfriend, who seemed to love being with him every bit as much as he loved being with her, especially when they were naked! In short, he was thriving and could not have been happier.

Socially, Miles and Laura mostly chummed with Jo, Delores and Jill. In the autumn of '83, the five of them celebrated Thanksgiving at the Needler's cottage. Since the three ladies had slaved all day to cook a delicious turkey feast, Miles and Jo insisted on doing the dishes. Gleefully freed from domestic duties, Jill and Delores escorted their lovely host to the cellar vault, where they selected a bottle of fine wine.

When the cousins were finished cleaning the kitchen, they joined the women in the living room. The capacious sitting area was heated by the crackling flames of two fires, via a woodstove at one end of the room and a fireplace at the other. Jo sat on the sofa between his two girlfriends; Laura parked herself on Miles's knee as he sat in an oversized armchair.

Laura proclaimed the '76 bottle of merlot to be an excellent vintage. After a sip, she spoke of its cherry-cedar aroma and chewy, rustic aftertaste. Delores said to her, "Where'd you learn to describe wine like that?"

"My mother has been a connoisseur for as long as I can remember."

Jill smacked remnants of merlot grape between her lips. "Can't put my finger on it but there's something about the taste of this wine that's mighty familiar."

As part of an ongoing joke that exemplified Miles's new prowess with the English language, Jo said to the girls, "Who has a question for *The Scholar*?"

Jill raised her hand in jest. "How would The Scholar describe his girlfriend?" (Jo was surprised by the hot-blooded spirit she had asked the question, as if challenging Miles to adequately praise the raven haired beauty.)

"Do you want a wholesome or spicy version?" Miles said.

"Oh, make it spicy, Miles," Jill said, "For sure, hot and spicy!"

Miles thought for a few seconds then cleared his throat: "Laura's pelf of pulchritude culminates in the chewy, rustic aftertaste of her protuberant pudenda!"

Jo doubled over with a cackle of laughter! Delores said, "Pelf of pulchritude? What's that mean, Jo?"

"It means wealth of beauty."

"Miles," Jill said, "I understand you were comparing Laura to the fine wine we're drinking—very clever—but what does 'protuberant pudenda' mean?"

"I was referring to her thick, luscious lips."

"That's nice Miles," Jill said, "But I thought you were going to give us the 'spicy version.'"

"Uh," Jo said, "He was referring to her *lower lips*."

Delores broke into a paroxysm of laughter. "He thinks Laura has a chewy, rustic aftertaste…*down there*?"

Laura slapped Miles on his chest. Jo's laughter subsided when he realized Jill was in the throes of a racy crush on Laura!

Jill said to Miles, "Besides a lot of weird words, what else have you been learning at university?"

"Believe it or not, I had to read a romance novel for a humanities class. Swollen member this, swollen member that; if a man has an erection, he's instantly a member of the swollen member club! (Everyone laughed except for Jill.) Apparently, the author used euphemisms to make sex seem more palatable. To me, the purple prose watered down the sensuality with unintentional hilarity.

"I also found the characters too perfect, too syrupy to be true. For instance, the main protagonist, Hope, describes Christopher as 'Unbelievably beautiful, almost too good looking!' Yet, she wears her independence like armour to repel his charms. He wins Hope over, however, by flying her in his private jet, on a mission to feed starving children in Africa!" Miles ran his fingers through Laura's hair and added, "Guess an average looking guy from a middle class family, could never win the heart of a beautiful woman."

(Jill thought, *in your case, a blind woman who can't see what you look like*!)

"I used to read romance novels," Laura said, "In retrospect, it seems to me the genre was bent on justifying women's natural sexuality."

"What do you mean, Laura?" Jill asked.

"Well, if a woman is known to have a healthy sex drive, that is, if she loves sex, then society often labels her a 'slut.' But if the female protagonist in a romance novel has sex with someone like Christopher, a 'hunk' who helps feed starving children in Africa, then her sex drive is suddenly justified and acceptable. Why can't women do what comes naturally, without having to worry about certain criteria imposed by society?"

"I agree" Jill said, "In certain instances, a woman doesn't need a man to do what comes naturally!"

After they all laughed, Delores said, "But romance novels promote the tender, loving side of relationships. Is that so terrible?"

"It's not that I'm against romance, per se," Miles said, "You all know how I met Laura at the quarry. Still, you can't deny base needs are behind every red rose, every candlelit dinner. And let's face it, there are times when a man wants to just throw it into a woman and a woman wants to have it thrown into her!"

"I can't believe you Miles!" Jill said, "One minute you're talking like a pompous professor, the next minute you sound like a foul mouthed trucker!"

"I think Miles and Laura have made interesting points," Jo said, "Physical attraction is obviously important; but nobody can make love every second of every day. Besides raw lust, there's companionship and caring for a loved one when she's ill. Perhaps there's no limit to the manner in which people can love each other."

They all agreed with Jo. Delores planted a lingering kiss upon his lips...then kissed Jill with equal fervour. It was the first time Miles had seen two women making out like that, found it titillating…till he saw Jill flash such a sultry glance at Laura, he got flustered! "Uh, who wants to play SCRABBLE?" he said.

They went to the kitchen table and set up Laura's braille version of the game. In the hush of concentration, Laura's thoughts strayed to the poem Jo had written her back in high school. She'd never mentioned the love letter to either cousin because she didn't want to cause conflict between them. She couldn't help wonder, however, how it might have been if she'd become involved with Jo back then.

Whoa! Jo thought, Jill's infatuated with Laura while Laura contemplates my long, lost letter! How can I fix this? In the game, he played the word "pickle."

Miles laid down "khat" and Jill broke the silence with a sudden cackle. "What are you trying to pull, Miles? There's no such word!"

"So you're challenging me?" he said in a tone that bordered on cockiness.

She picked up the dictionary and ravaged its pages. "I'll be damned—it's a shrub used in tea!" She lost her turn.

When it came around to Miles's turn again, he played "dhow."

"*Dhow*?" Jill lashed out. "*Are you dcrazy*?"

Miles smiled. "Do you really want to risk losing your turn again?"

"What does it mean then?"

"Don't know, really. A boat or a piece of clothing maybe."

"If you don't know what it means, you can't use it—lose your turn!"

"Show me in the rules where it says you have to define the words you use."

Jill scanned the rules on the SCRABBLE box and found no such rule existed. "I don't care, you're bluffing—I'm challenging you anyway!"

She flipped through the dictionary and found "dhow." "Son of a B—it's a kind of a boat!"

Jo laughed. "That's what you get for messing with The Scholar!"

When it was Miles's turn again, Jill watched him like a hawk. He played a *c* and a *w* on top of an *m*.

"*CWM*?" Jill bellowed, "THERE'S NO VOWEL—ALL WORDS HAVE AT LEAST ONE VOWEL—PASS ME THE DICTIONARY!"

She scanned a page, came to the geological word "cwm," slammed the dictionary closed, then stormed off to bed.

Delores looked at Jo. "Should I go and talk to her?"

"Let's give her some time to cool down."

"I don't understand why she takes the game so serious," Laura said.

"I have a confession to make," Miles said. "Whenever I see a good SCRABBLE word in the dictionary, I jot it down. I have a huge list of words memorized. Hope I didn't cause too much trouble."

"I think it's great that you have such a passion for words," Laura said.

"Don't worry Miles," Delores said, "Jill just doesn't like to lose."

Jo wished it was that simple! The four remaining players finished the game. Despite Miles's quirky words, Laura won by five points. (Jo, of course, would never use his gift to beat his friends at a game.) They talked until midnight, then went to bed.

***

Naked beneath a silk sheet and cozy comforter, Miles and Laura had just started kissing and caressing when someone knocked on their door. "Yes?" Laura said.

Across the room from the foot of the bed, Jill opened the door and a hallway nightlight silhouetted a wispy nightie, draped upon her buff body. "I just wanted to say sorry for the way I acted this evening. Don't know what got into me."

"That's alright," Miles said, "Me and my crazy words."

With her head hung low, Jill glanced at them and said, "Guess I'll go back to bed then."

"Goodnight," Laura said.

Jill bowed out and closed the door.

Miles laughed. "What was that all about?"

"She wanted to join us."

"*In our bed*? Get out—no way!"

"I have to admit," she said, "the three of them get my curiosity going—the possibilities seem endless!"

"Really? You'd be into this sort of thing?"

She giggled. "You wouldn't be?"

"Just talking about it has swollen my member!"

She took hold of his hardness and said, "A member in good standing!"

"I stand on guard for thee!" They laughed so hard, one of them snorted! She said, "What would your favourite position be?"

"Let me see…I love it when you're on top because my hands are free to touch you all over, so one woman riding me while the other sits on my face."

"Would the two women be kissing?"

That was it! Miles ravished her with a fluent French tongue while his fingers explored the wetness of her thick folds. Inspired by his fantasy of a threesome, she sat on his face in a heated bout of 69. Then she straddled his hips. Amid her third orgasm, he came also, groaning so hard and long, he couldn't help add a little laughter, like a martyr in rapture, like revelry near death.

Breathless, she collapsed upon his chest. In the euphoria of afterglow, she said, "Amazing how a little fantasy can spice things up. Next time you'll have to tell me your favourite position for two men and a woman."

"*Doesn't work that way—only works with two women*!"

Laura laughed so hard she nearly fell out of bed! She then set her clock radio so they could fall asleep to a soft rock station. Miles drifted off to the sweet, whining coda of "Layla." Laura was about to do the same when a news bulletin terrified her fully awake: an infamous local boy had escaped the Millhaven Pen.

***

The next morning, Jo didn't want to wake anyone (especially Jill) by flushing the toilet, so he went outside in his sweatshirt and boxers to pee. As he relieved himself beneath the autumnal, red leaves of a maple tree, he perceived a wicked wave of spleen. He tucked his penis back into his boxers, then turned to face Dave Needler.

"You just couldn't *fucking* leave her alone!" he said, as he pointed a revolver.

Jo thought Needler's black eye patch made his functional eye all the more piercing. And something about the self-assured manner in which he wore his green prison uniform suggested he was king amongst convicts.

"If you make a sound," Dave said, "I'll blow your head off! Follow the path to your left."

Jo knew he wasn't bluffing. As he walked with the gun jammed into his back, he saw a deep, dark hole in Needler's thoughts.

"You must be dense or something, "Dave said. "I mean, *I beat you into a coma* the last time you messed with my sister—I should've finished you off back then!"

They reached the hole Jo had seen in Dave's thoughts, an abandoned well, or maybe an old mineshaft, covered by three 2X6 planks. Dave waved his gun at the boards and ordered Jo to remove them.

"Guess I can't blame you for holding a grudge," Jo said, as he uncovered the hole. "You were only trying to protect your sister."

"No point sucking up to me now, not after you fucked her—in our family's cabin no less!" He cocked his pistol. "What are you waiting for? Jump!"

"A true executioner always grants last words."

As Jo expected, Dave loved hearing himself referred to as an executioner, the power over life and death made him feel like a god. "Okay Martini, I'll bite: Any last words?"

"I realize brothers can be protective of their sisters, but isn't this a bit extreme?"

"Entire countries have gone to war over women as beautiful as Laura. Killing a piece of shit like you means nothing! Anything else?"

Jo could only think of one other question that might extend his life a few moments longer. "How could you sleep with your own sister?"

"What? How'd you—SHE'S NOT MY REAL SISTER, MORON!"

"But still."

"Martini, I live by principles you couldn't possibly understand; but since it's part of your final request, I'll try to explain. The best is the best—*Laura is the absolute best!* She happens to be my stepsister—so what? Nobody could ever take her place. Understand, sport? Now, I've answered your stupid ass questions. No more stalling. Jump—or I'll blow your head off!"

Jo figured his only chance for survival was to make a run for it. Perhaps the gun would misfire. Even if it did go off, Dave might miss.

The desperate clairvoyant was about to bolt when he sensed a third party. "Jo, don't jump!" Laura cried out.

Dave lowered his gun. "Laura! What are you doing here?"

Dressed in a grey sweat suit, she tapped her cane along the edge of the path, tripped over an aboveground root, jumped back to her feet; tripped over a stone, got right back up again. Finally, she stepped up to her stepbrother. "I heard on the radio you had escaped. When Jo didn't return to the cabin, I assumed the worst and, well, here you are."

"I busted out of prison—pretty cool, eh?"

"How'd you pull that off?"

"Compromised a guard—made him an offer he couldn't refuse!"

"Tell me something Dave, were you responsible for the 'prom bomb'?"

"I couldn't stand the thought of you being there without me, dancing with some jerk-off while I was stuck in prison. When you survived, I realized fate was on our side, we were meant to be together—and here we are! Let me get rid of this loser and—"

"Hold on Dave, Jo hasn't done anything wrong. Let him go."

"But he's obsessed with you! Remember the letter he left in your locker?"

"Jo is just a friend. We're not together the way you think. Jeez, you really do care for me—I never realized how much until this very second."

"Think I'm stupid? You're just saying that so I don't *off your boyfriend.*"

"I already told you, he's just a friend." She reached out and grabbed her stepbrother's arm. "Nobody will understand you the way I do. Remember how our parents always took off on us? We only ever had each other."

"So it wasn't just the thing that happened in Mexico. We fell in love—for real!"

"Sorry it took me so long to accept it." (Jo knew what she was up to and it terrified him!)

"Where can we go from here?" Dave said, "Our families will never accept us being together. Then there's this fugitive thing I got going. I'm never going back to prison—can't stand to be away from you ever again!"

She stroked his arm. "There is a way we could be together forever, without worrying about prison or the world at large."

"What do you mean?"

"Do you really want to be with me forever?"

"It's all I've ever wanted."

Laura locked her arm with his, in the classic escort position. She inched Dave to the brink of the pit. He inadvertently kicked a pebble into the hole; they heard it bounce off ledges, but never heard it hit bottom.

"I get it," Dave said, "We'll be together for all eternity!"

"Like Romeo and Juliet," she added. "At the count of three: ONE, TWO, THREE…"

As Dave jumped, Laura spun a half pirouette, wrenching her arm free from his—but lost her balance and slipped off the edge! Jo dove to the ground and snatched her wrist before she disappeared into the dark abyss. The momentum of her dragged him forward till his toes hooked onto a cedar root, sprawled above the forest floor. The last thoughts Jo heard from Dave were a series of expletives the madman failed to scream out loud, because shock and rage had choked off his vocal cords.

With adrenaline fuelled strength, Jo hauled Laura up and out of the hole. Sitting safely on solid ground, Laura latched onto him and said, “I’m so sorry.”

“It’s not your fault. He was mad about you, literally insane!”

“I wonder how he knew about the letter you wrote me back in high school. He must have salvaged it from the garbage after I threw it away. Creepy how he kept tabs on me.” She hesitated, then added, “I’ve been meaning to thank you for the poem. Sorry I didn’t appreciate at the time. I was a different person back then. If only—”

“Things worked out for the best, Laura—you and Miles are great together!”

“That’s true. I never imagined I could be this happy. Jo, let’s not tell anyone what happened here this morning. I don’t want to waste another second of my life dealing with my maniacal brother.”

“You had a brother?”

She smiled and kissed him on the cheek. He led her back to the cottage. They slipped inside as everyone else was starting to stir.

At breakfast, Jill’s mood was worse than the night before. Exacerbating the situation, her infatuation with Laura began to irk Delores. And then, adding even more tension, Miles said, “Jo, would you mind telling me what you were doing with Laura this morning—outside in your underwear?”

Jill did a double take of Jo and Laura. “Really Miles, you saw them together?”

“I saw them through my bedroom window.”

"Don't worry Miles," Laura said, "Let me have a word with you in private."

Reluctantly, he led her to the bedroom. A few minutes later, Miles returned with bounce in his step. "I have an announcement to make: I'm moving in with Laura! Sorry for snapping at you, Jo. Laura explained how she followed you outside to ask your opinion about us living together. Thanks for encouraging her to go ahead with it. For an obvious reason, she didn't know you were in your boxers."

Jo and Delores congratulated the happy couple; Jill stormed off to pack!

Chapter Twenty-two

When Miles moved into the Needler mansion, Betty was furious! She lectured him about "shacking up" (some shack!), imploring him to abide by the Holy Sacrament of marriage. But Miles and Laura believed they didn't need a contract to prove they loved each other.

After months of harassment, however, the young couple relented, agreeing to get married in December, during Miles's Christmas break. They had only one condition: the dress code for their celebration had to be casual. In their opinion, pro-movement, ultra-comfortable clothing would diffuse some of the tension inherent in weddings. Appalled, Betty objected vehemently!

Three nights before her son's "big day," Betty called him for the umpteenth time. Miles hung up on her. Betty said to Anton, "Drive me there—NOW!"

"It's *their* wedding," Anton said, "why don't you leave them alone?"

"YOU'RE EITHER WITH ME OR AGAINST ME!"

Before long, Betty was pounding the heavy oak door at her son's stately abode. Miles refused to answer. Laura said, "Do you really want to shut your mother out like this?"

"There was a time when she dominated me and there was nothing I could do about it—those days are over!"

Betty continued to make a ruckus outdoors. "This is ridiculous," Laura said, "I'm letting her in!"

"If you open that door, I'll walk out and never come back!"

"Okay Miles, take it easy—no need to get crazy!"

"Sorry, but Betty can bring out the worst of me."

"Miles, why don't we skip the wedding and go straight to the honeymoon?"

"Really?"

"This ordeal with your mother has convinced me we should have trusted our instincts. I don't need a contract to prove I love you—I want to prove it every day!"

"Darlin', I *love* the way you think! Let's not tell Betty—she'd freak!"

"I'll check with my mom's travel agent and see if we can leave a day early."

Since the Needlers had been frequent flyers for years, the travel agent was happy to accommodate the honeymooners by bumping up their itinerary. Anton didn't blame his son for leaving. He kept warning Betty to back off, but she wouldn't listen. In the absence of a wedding, Anton held a house party to honour the young couple's continued happiness. Miles and Laura weren't the only absentees; dismayed by her son's "abandonment," Betty refused to come out of her room.

And Jo Martini was single again, his relationship with Jill and Delores torn asunder! Unable to cope with her hopeless love for Laura, the brawny construction worker moved to Montreal. Delores then became inconsolable, the mere site of Jo a constant reminder of Jill and the ecstasy of how they used to be. Falling into a deep depression, Delores moved back in with her parents. Jo believed the break-up was for the best. Since joining Canada's secret service, the wily clairvoyant didn't have enough time for a conventional relationship, let alone a three-way.

By 10 p.m, Anton was feeling no pain, *feeling no wife*. Serving drinks from behind his rec room bar, he had met several of his son's classmates, as well as Laura's friends from the Institute for the Blind.

When Jo approached the bar, Anton opened a cold beer for him and said, "Where are your lovely girlfriends this evening?"

"As it turned out uncle Anton, cohabitating with Jill and Delores was like living in a house of cards, not very stable for the long run."

"House of cards? Ha! Try living in a house full of flying battleaxes!"

Reluctantly, Jo shared a laugh with his uncle.

"Uh, that wasn't nice. Your aunt's not so bad. Just a little headstrong."

"A successful marriage seems to have more to do with stability than anything else. Since you and aunt Betty have been married for almost thirty years, the two of you must be doing something right."

"I suppose you're right…you sure know how to put a positive spin on things!" He raised his cocktail glass and clinked it against Jo's beer bottle.

Harrietta approached the bar. "Which one of you handsome devils wants to dance with me?"

Anton volunteered in earnest. Two songs later, Ana sent Igor to cut in. Jo thought, good move mom: That's all we'd need is for aunt Betty to join the party, only to find her husband dancing with another woman—a beautiful one at that!

Epilogue

Originally, Miles wanted to honeymoon somewhere tropical, perhaps Mexico; but Laura, who'd been skiing since she was six, insisted on a trip to Banff. They started on bunny hills with Miles acting as her eyes. Before long, they cruised down intermediate slopes.

Most of the time, however, they stayed in their rented cabin, warmed by a crackling fire, as Laura tantalized Miles with her recent penchant for dressing up and role playing. Her clothing fetish started when she realized wearing high heeled shoes to bed didn't hurt her back, knees or feet. Her passion for fashion, what she used to live for, thus found a new outlet—*all those years in vogue gone racy rogue!*

On her first night in Banff, Laura donned a wedding veil, a bodice with garters, lacy stockings and white high heels. Her bridal lingerie turned Miles on so much, he went down on her for over an hour!

Maintaining her wedding theme on their second night, Laura dressed as a stripper, donning black stockings and knee-high boots, teasing the dickens out of Miles while dancing for his make believe stag.

On the fourth night, however, Miles was confused when she came out of the bedroom in a gaudy, burgundy gown. She thinks *this* is sexy? But then she lifted the bottom of her gown, slowly, revealing a pair of satin, come-fuck-me high heels, and sheer nude stockings clipped to a garter belt.

Without hesitation, he bent her over the dresser and took her from behind. She eventually finished him off with the best blowjob of his young life! While catching her breath, Laura said, "What'd you think?"

"Fantastic! Nasty, horny bridesmaid, right?"

"Yes—terribly jealous of the bride!"

***

The young lovers awoke one morning to a blue truth: honeymoons don't last forever. After a late checkout, Miles drove their rented Mercedes east along the Trans-Canada Highway. As he described the scenery, his enthusiasm for snow capped peaks and breathtaking precipices put Laura in the mood.

At her behest, Miles meandered along a back road, into the Seven Sisters mountain range, where he parked in a picnic area closed for the season. After obliging Laura's insatiable libido, he slipped out of her without a climax of his own. "That was beautiful, Love" he said, "but now we'll miss our flight and I have a class in the morning!" She pleaded with him to slip back inside her to finish what they had started; but he refused her—for the first time—dressed in a hurry, and sped out from between the legs of the Seven Sisters.

***

Laura tapped her cane feverishly through the Calgary Airport, as Miles guided her through a maze of hangar-like corridors. They reached their gate as an attendant was closing the ramp door. Once settled in their seats, he cuddled his arm around her and she nestled her cheek into the nook between his shoulder and chest. Moments after takeoff, they fell into a deep sleep.

Most everyone has had the dream where they're falling. For Laura, it's a hellish drop in the clutches of a maniac. Miles also had a nightmare: after an operation restored Laura's vision, she took one look at him and sent him packing—as if regaining her sight would reinstate her as the Cleopatra of Kingston, the haughty and heartless queen of mean!

He awoke to her fingertips caressing his chest under his sweater. "I had a bad dream," she said, "Could you take me to the restroom, so I can freshen up?"

After he led her to the loo, she stepped inside and pulled him in! While becoming a member of the mile high club, he felt in his heart it wasn't just lust; for when they parted in his dream, what he missed most was holding her close. During her murmurs of rapture, amid the muffled roar of the plane, he took great comfort in confirming, yet again, Laura was the absolute mistress of his heart.